The Amulet of Kings

Will Macmillan Jones

First published in 2011 by Safkhet Publishing

Second edition 2016 by Red Kite Publishing Limited

www.redkitepublishing.net

Text Copyright 2011 by Will Macmillan Jones

Will Macmillan Jones asserts the moral right to be identified as the author of this work under the Copyright, Designs and Patents Act 1988.

All characters and events in this publication other than those clearly in the public domain, are fictitious and any resemblance to real persons, living or dead, is purely coincidental.

All rights reserved. No part of this publication may be reproduced, stored in or introduced into a retrieval system, or transmitted, in any form or by any means, including but not limited to electronic, mechanical, photocopying or recording, without the prior written permission of the publisher.

A CIP catalogue record for this book is available from the British Library.

ISBN:
978-1523895243

Author's introduction to the second edition

We want to re issue Amulet of Kings, with the original text, said the Publishers.

I'd like to revise it to make it better, now that I've got a few years experience under my belt, I said.

No, the original text, warts and all, they insisted.

I really want to make it into the book I'd always dreamed about, to reflect who I am and what I do now, I replied.

No, the original text is what we want, they told me.

Over my dead body! I told them.

Maybe that comment needs re evaluating so as to continue to express the overall concept whilst maintaining a less rigorous emphasis on the literal and specific content of the remarks, I told their hitman when he called.

So here it is. As it was originally. For posterior. Or maybe posterity. Whatever. I haven't touched it, except to remove the dedication. No, not even that. Honest.

CONTENTS

	Dedication	V
1	Chapter One	Pg 3
2	Chapter Two	Pg 17
3	Chapter Three	Pg 31
4	Chapter Four	Pg 44
5	Chapter Five	Pg 63
6	Chapter Six	Pg 87
7	Chapter Seven	Pg 116
8	Chapter Eight	Pg 138
9	Chapter Nine	Pg 171
10	Chapter Ten	Pg 192
11	Chapter Eleven	Pg 223
12	Chapter Twelve	Pg 238

DEDICATION

When asked by the publisher if I wanted to write a dedication for this book, there could only be one answer: the characters, and in particular The Banned Underground. Led by a jazz-loving bogtroll, this bunch of drunken, pizza loving dwarfs shouldered their way into my head; and as so often with unwanted guests had a riotous party and forgot that they had homes of their own waiting for them.

Of course the real inspiration came first from the incomparable delight of rambling in the Lake District: sitting beside the Boulder Stone, panting on the steep slopes of mighty Helvellyn, gasping at the view from the easier to reach Cat Bells and lying under a brilliant blue sky on top of the sprawling High street (site of the highest known Roman Road in the world) dreaming of a whole land of elves, dwarfs, trolls and wizards living and laughing and squabbling all around us and below the soul-searing beauty of the high fells. Who could sit there and not want to write about it?

And the music. Always, at the heart of it, the music. Has it been a long time since Rock N Roll? Not for The Banned Underground. It's never been away.

This is the story of a time in the history of an Amulet. NOT a charm, which can be, well, a bit charming – a bit lightweight in magical terms. The impression to get is of the sort of thing that needs a very thick chain to hang from. And a very thick neck to hang around. HRH King Kong would do nicely, here. Solid. Dependable. Worthy.

Which is why it was such a shame that it was lost one night after a rather good party

Following a concert by the Banned Underground, a mystical Rhythm & Blues band.

Cover Artwork sponsored by Grizelda's Frog Sanctuary.

CHAPTER ONE

Robert Smith and his Band The Cure are in love with Friday. They made a hit record about it.

Sir Bob Geldof doesn't like Mondays. He, too, wrote a hit record about it.

Grizelda, Witch of the Fourth Pentangle, didn't like any day of the week very much but lacked the commercial skill to exploit the song and dance she made about it.

In fact, her lack of commercial skill was a problem, as it meant that for the fourth year running she had failed to make the Joint Convention for White Witches and Wizards of Caer Rigor, and Black Witches, Wizards and Warlocks of Caer Surdin. Held in the South of France, again. The conference was held jointly to save money, and because it saved having to fight each other in the good weather.

[Grizelda, despite the colour of her laundry, and especially despite her kitchen, was nominally a member of the White Group. Although her membership was occasionally reviewed for excessive use of her frog/people spell.]

This late afternoon was dark, very dark. So dark that the wind kept bumping into things, which occasionally fell over. To ease the fears of environmentalists at this point, the wind was unharmed. Rain fell, driven in sheets by the wind, on anything that moved. Or didn't move, rain having signed a non discrimination agreement.

All things considered, Grizelda was not in a good temper. Aggravated, multiplied by very, very cross sums it up well. So when her broomstick began to misfire, and the terrain clearance fell to roughly six inches unless the power cut in or she lifted her skirts over a particularly large rock (which resulted in some spectacular if unplanned aerobatics) it is safe to presume her mood did not improve. Trailing skeins of green smoke, the witch progressed erratically across the heather with one hand on her hat for security and the other on her skirts for modesty. She would have been better off if she had had three hands – for example, she might have been able to steer.

"Its no fun on your own," she muttered. "Can't go round saying 'When shall we meet again?' Not when there's only one of you, and the cat, and about 600 cat fleas. Not even easy to 'ave a good row. Not impossible, just not easy." But then, a wild, eldritch screech to freeze the blood burst from her lips – "TOURISTS!"

Away in the rain haunted mist she could see some hikers trudging through the gathering storm towards the village, in the hope that it represented if not safety, then at least the chance to be robbed in the dry. The witch narrowed her eyes, shifted her grip on the broomstick...

"AAAAAAAAAAAAAAAAAAAAAAAAHHHHHHHHHHHHH!" she screamed as she and the broomstick swapped places relative to the ground.

"AAAAAAAAAAAAAAAAAAAAAAAAHHHHHHHHHHHHH!" screamed a hiker, as crockery used earlier in her picnic fell from Grizelda's pockets and showered around the hiker's head. "FLYING SAUCERS!"

"Little green men?" asked her companion, with visions from various sci-fi movies running through his head.

[These usually involved an attractive female lead being abducted and ravished by unbelievably good-looking aliens, and kept several psychiatrists from enjoying their just rewards on Jobseekers Allowance.]

"No," answered the first hiker. "It was black, upside down and threw these at me." She held up a cheap dinner plate inscribed with archaic lettering, which read : "Virgin Rail".

"Interstellar travellers, eh?" mused the second hiker. "Must be bloody rich if they can afford to use the trains to get around when they get here. And no wonder they never arrive when you expect them, either. Instead of sneaking around in clouds trying to avoid the RAF, they are probably sat on the platform at Crewe Station waiting for the connection to Venus and stealing souvenirs from the buffet to laugh at when they get home."

"Got to be better than *eating* the food I suppose."

Aloft, Grizelda nursed the failing broomstick to cloud base (30 feet), surrounded by green fumes from the back end, which made her look like a small, bilious cumulus cloud. Muttering curses, which missed and so didn't help her quota, she headed home. Landings could be tricky...

"OK, Approach speed 1.3 times stalling speed... Flaps down.." She dropped her skirts and undid her coat.... "Here Goessssssss..."

Climbing out of the compost heap she swore, and then swore to get a newer model...

*

Manchester was busy. The day was fine, so instead of sheltering from the rain, the pickpockets and muggers were out and about, practising their viable alternative to paid employment. Our vision is guided to the South of the City, and focuses now on one particular house. Within, life was busy too, although muggings were unlikely as the weekly pocket money had been paid on time. Pocket picking of course remained an option.

"Now, with yer mother ill in hospital after visiting Leeds, there is no way I am going to... can *manage* to look after you. Playing in a bear pit, or going to Manchester United's football ground in a Manchester City scarf would be safer. So, you are both going to stop with your Aunt Dot in The Lake District for the holidays. No option."

A middle-aged father was lecturing his two sullen looking children. It would be tempting at this point to describe the father as tall, moderately good-looking, and an honest and upright person.* Unfortunately he was none of these things, so that temptation can be safely resisted.

[*Attributes of the typical Mancunian.]

The children were in their early teens, and therefore inclined to be moody. The elder of the two, Chris, was trying (though in fact failing) to look dark and interesting like a Northern Marlon Brando, whilst his slightly younger sister, Linda, was still in her tomboy phase. And blonde, another temptation to be resisted.

Both were tall and skinny. The prospect of a holiday in one of the few areas of the UK perceived to have a higher annual rainfall than Manchester seemed to lack appeal to the adolescents.

"Dad, are you trying to get rid of us?" asked Chris.

"No, of course not. I've succeeded."

"Yeah, but why there? It's all full of spiders and creepy things."

"One of those is Aunt Dot," complained Linda.

"But there's nothing to do, Dad!" added Chris.

"Yes there is, cleaning up after yer aunt for one thing. I still remember the last time she visited here. Took me ages to shift that last spider."

"Is he serious, Linda? I mean, it's miles to Macdonalds, and the telly is only black and green."

"Like yer aunt then," said their dad.

"She's got some creepy horrors there too," complained Linda.

"That's just her mates," replied her dad. "You should hear what people say about some of your mates. Better yet, perhaps, they should hear it. Anyway, it will be an experience for you. You'll come back changed kids."

"Yes," replied Chris. "Changed into frogs, probably."

"Well, she's the only one prepared to have you."

"For tea?"

"To stay. Anyway, she's turned the goat out to make room, so you two: just be grateful."

"For a month in an open prison?" sulked Linda.

"It's not open. She's had glass put in the windows now. Anyway, the taxi is here in twenty minutes, so get packing."

"Can't we visit Mum again before we go?" asked Linda.

"The doctors want her to get better. So no visits, they told me."

*

"Right," said the taxi driver. "That's as far as I can be bribed to go."

"But the house is right down that lane!" muttered Chris.

The teenagers stared down the lane. It was narrow, and unkempt, with weeds growing in the verges. Brought up in Manchester, they were unused to such things, the colour green being normally reserved for graffiti, and growing things for the car parks.

"Yep. But, your Auntie, she's not keen on taxi drivers. The last one to go down there never made it back." The driver leant closer to the kids. "But his ghost wanders the lanes, calling as a dreadful warning his last words..."

The teenagers, well versed in horror movies, shivered. What could they be?

"Oi! Where's me tip you witch?"

Chris and Linda sat down on their bags as the taxi vanished in an evil smelling cloud, as though the driver had diluted the petrol with something cheap and nasty. Canned lager? All around, clouds rested on the fells, taking a break from dropping rain on the lakes. In front of them, the lane wound south towards the lake, and a small dark cottage that stood on the banks. Chris sighed, and picked up their bags. "Let's get it over with."

Linda nodded.

"Gest.. Gerrrt,, Get wha' over?" slurred a voice beside them The children jumped round. A youth peered over the wall next to them, then very slowly fell over into a small but smelly peat bog in the next field. "Bin tryin' to get this peat to burn," he explained moodily. "The Scots an' Irish do it, so why not me?"

"Is it the right sort of peat?" asked Linda, bemused.

"Dunno. Should have asked it, I suppose. Still, can't expect a bit of bog to tell you straight if you can set fire to it. I'm Ned."

"I'm Chris, that's Linda, and you're drunk."

"No, I'm Ned. Just said that. Bloody kids, never listen. Where are you goin' then?"

"Down to the cottage."

"Oh, don't be doin' that. That Grotbags, she don't like visitors."

"Why?"

"They don't fry properly, I suppose. And turnin' them into frogs doesn't help. And what she did to the milkman, well it were horrible."

"What did she do?" asked Chris, fascinated.

"Well, she told him the milk were off. Then, when he tried to charge her anyway, she cursed him!"

"What did she do?" Chris wanted to know.

"She put spell on him, so he had ter be nice to people. See, it were all right with his customers, but when he went home and was nice ter his wife, well she wouldn't stand it. One thing kissing the customers, she said, but I'm not havin' yer come home and kissing me." With a mighty heave, Ned got his arms and shoulders over the wall, and treated the children to a gaze, which would have brought tears of joy to any shareholder in Guinness. With a shrug, Chris started down the lane. Linda looked back at Ned.

"Why do you call her Grotbags?"

"The way she dresses." Ned fell back off the wall, and lay there looking like an extra in a disaster movie – after the big scene." Don't say I didn't warn yer!" he called, scrabbling frantically for his pipe as it settled into the peat. "Keep getting bogged down in detail," he grumbled to himself.

"So there you are at last! You didn't have to be so loud," scolded Aunt Dot, opening the door to the cottage.

"But we only just opened the garden gate," explained Linda.

"That's no excuse. I nearly ruined an important test. If I had, you two would have had no tea!"

"Why?" asked Linda, who was hungry.*

[* A default state in teenagers.]

"Cos it was the curry sauce. Explosive sometimes. Come inside, and take care of the goat."

"Why?" asked Linda, again.

"Cos he's just road tested the curry, and might need some room to move."

"Do goats move fast?" asked Chris.

"They do if you put a lit match near their whatsit after a plate of vindaloo. You are having the same rooms, the crocodile is quite safe now, the second taxidermist got it properly stuffed at last."

"What with?"

"The first taxidermist, mostly. When you come down, Chris, you can get the fire lit."

Later, with the fire lit and the washing up safely ignored, the three sat by the open window listening to the evening sounds of the small night time creatures going about their business, and the goat's stomach complaining about the curry. The two children stared at their aunt, who had changed little since their last visit. Just above medium height (if you have an average sized medium of course: the ones who perform on TV always seem to be a bit tall), with long tangled dark hair and clothes that had certainly seen better days, and quite a few better nights as well, she was almost a classic modern version of the traditional forest witch.

Of course, to get Council Building Regulations approval for the cottage she had had to give up on the gingerbread and marzipan as building materials, and she had also cut down on the straw roof (in that case however because the local thatcher was too expensive). But the oven door still shut with a traditional clang and the kitchen remained a place to avoid on safety grounds, not least as a result of the smell, which contravened some important Biological Warfare Treaties. The sitting room was however comfortably furnished, with a pleasant open fire in the grate and a nice sofa. Occasional chairs also graced the room, and were occasionally sat on by the brave. Prints of elderly relatives, and occult icons hung on the walls, and sometimes it was hard to tell the difference.

"So, how's yer mum?" asked their aunt.

"Supposed to be getting better, but they won't let us visit her," complained Linda, who was missing her mother.

"That'll be 'cos they want her to get well enough to leave hospital. Don't expect me sister gives the nurses an easy time."

"She doesn't give us an easy time, so why should the doctors get one?" muttered Chris.

"Where's Uncle Ben?" asked Linda.

"Dunno," her aunt replied. "Sent him off to do an errand this afternoon, and I suppose he met some of his mates. They don't seem to like me much. Can't abide intolerance."

Linda looked at Chris. That was a bit rich, coming from someone who turned visitors into frogs instead of saying 'Go Away'. Linda picked up a somewhat faded photo of her Uncle. He was dressed simply, in a tatty monk's cloak (a bad habit he had picked up on his travels) and the angle of the photo emphasised that he was tall, craggily good looking and had a mild expression. (Which could turn bitter if he had too much to drink) She knew him as good-natured, but reserved, like an old port. [Probably not Grimsby. Certainly not Hull.]

"He'll be back," said Dot comfortably." And he'd better have what I sent him to the shops for."

"But it's late," said Linda." Shouldn't we be worried?"

"Too much like hard work," muttered her aunt.

"I tried hard work, but it doesn't agree with me," put in Chris.

The two females looked unconvinced. To the teenagers' unease, their aunt leant back in her chair and, her eyes closed, started snorting like a steam train. Nothing magical happened. Instead of entering an eldritch trance, she had dozed off. Linda stood up, and walked to the window. Night was falling, and she could no longer see across the garden, although several of the plants could see her and waved.

"Bit rude," remarked a rambling rose as Linda turned away without waving back.

"Kids today," replied the foxglove.

Chris stood up and turned on the lamp. "Nice shade."

"Yeah. Why is it always skulls and bats?"

Unseen, outside, a dark cowl lifted gingerly over a selected part of the wall, and sniffed carefully. It paused, and then came the sound of someone being colourfully sick. The cowl, now decorated with an interesting pattern, rose over a different part of the wall, and vaulted lightly over... into a patch of nettles.

A second cowl appeared." Pillock!" it hissed. "Here we are, stealing menacingly into a witch's garden, and you make more noise than a camel looking at two bricks!"

"Uhn. Sorry, Ned," grunted the first cowl, a junior wizard in spite of his older years. "But you made me take me boots off to be quiet, and she's planted nettles everywhere!"

"Shuurup." Ned, now revealed as the second cowl, jumped over the wall, avoiding the nettles by landing on the first cowl, and then jumping onto the grass.

Back inside the cottage, Aunt Dot was waking up. "All is Dark!" she exclaimed.

"Yes, auntie, it's night time."

"That's not what I meant. There is a strong force keeping Ben from coming home."

"Newcastle Brown Ale?"

"I'll have to go and look for him." Aunt Dot fussed around the room, putting on two coats before finally dragging an enormous pair of boots over to her chair, and with some difficulty lacing her feet into them. Outside, the two cowled figures stole across the garden. Well, one of them stole. The other hopped awkwardly on one leg.

"Can't you even creep properly!" complained Ned.

"Sorry, Brother. It's them nettles. Why can't I wear me boots? Cost me a weeks wages, they did."

"If yer can't creep, stalk."

"Stalkin's Chapter Four, we don't do than till next month."

"Shut up. The door's opening, get in that shadow, quick!"

The cottage door opened and Aunt Dot emerged. Slowly, weighted down by the boots, she stamped down the path muttering about the costs of servicing the broomstick at Dwarves R Us, and her husband getting drunk again. In the shadows by the wall, something stirred. A wavering shape raised its arms, drew away from the building... threw back the cowl and tripped over a piece of garden hose discarded by the goat as inedible... stumbled forward fighting for balance... stepped on the wrong end of a rusting rake and collapsed as the handle rose from the inky night and slapped it round the head. Aunt Dot's low-tech external security had worked efficiently.

"Ned! Ned!" whispered the junior wizard, urgently. "Are you OK?"

"Sometimes," groaned Ned from a dark area near the wall that smelt of cat, goats droppings and Guinness, "I find it hard to express my feelings in words."

The junior crouched down in the darkness next to Ned. "Me brother knows one of them psychiatrists. He said it made you feel better to express your feelings in any way you can."

Ned rose from the floor, and kicked the junior wizard hard between the legs and then as he fell over, on the side of the head." Mind you," continued the smitten one, "he always was a pillock."

"Oh, I dunno. I feel better anyhow."

Aunt Dot turned back. "Who's there? If you're from the Council, I'll pay me poll tax when I get a bloody parrot, and not before." She glared through the dusk. "Oh, it's you two numpties again, from the Watches. Get lost, go back to your boss an' tell him I'm getting fed up with you. Bog Off!"

The two shapes limped off down the path. At the gate, one turned and made a mystical invocation involving two fingers, only to find Uncle Ben arriving out of the dark to express his feelings (non verbally) with an empty beer bottle he just happened to have about him at the time.

"Sorry I'm late, luv. Stopped off down the pub, after shopping," called Ben. "These cause any aggro?"

"Nah, their too daft yet. Really, I don't mind. At least they know I exist, not like some of my lot."

"Oh don't start again. You know yer wouldn't like the Mediterranean. It's so hot yer would have to take off your boots, an' at least one coat."

As they walked back up the path, neither Ben nor Aunt Dot saw the curtains fall back into place as the two teenagers stepped back from the window.

CHAPTER TWO

People say dawn comes too soon. Dawn disagrees. If humans would just have a standard internal time, then life would be so much easier; timings could be adjusted to suit everyone. No one need be late (for work) again. Mind you, that would cause unreasonable unemployment amongst clock makers, and radio DJ s who make a living from being awake before everyone else at unreasonable times of the morning. Actually, maybe she has a point... Anyway, Dawn's early light streamed across the lake, and (with only a shudder of distaste,) touched the cottage. The children stirred.

"What's that awful smell?" asked Linda.

"I was going to ask that," said Chris.

"Sorry, must have been the curry," said the goat. Only in goatish. The children just heard a complicated bleat.

"Br-zen, Ick-zen," said Chris. The goat looked hurt, and remembering to open the window in order to preserve the new glass and important bits of its anatomy (at least the goat considered them important, and in this context his opinion counted), jumped out.

"The sound of two bricks clapping," said Chris, with a grin. "Aunt Dot taught me that one."

"Did she teach you anything else about goats?"
"Don't strike a match near its whatsit after it's had a curry."

Downstairs in the kitchen, a huge pot bubbled on the stove. Linda approached it with a set expression and a ladle.

17

"Take care, Linda. You don't know what's in there," warned Chris.

"Don't care. I'm hungry. If it doesn't move, I'm gonna eat it. In fact, even if it does move, but isn't that fast…"

"Don't touch that!" shouted Aunt Dot coming silently into the kitchen.

"What is it?"

"Your Uncle's socks!" A cloud of evil yellow gas roiled out of the pot and slunk around the kitchen ceiling, where even the spiders avoided it.

"Auntie," said Chris, "I think I'd like to go for a walk today."

"OK, but take a map, so as you can be sure you get back. And any walking stick *except* the one with a horses head handle."

"Why, is it magical?"

"Sort of. We use it to pull the goat out of the privy."

Aunt Dot glared at the yellow steam, until it looked embarrassed, and slunk back into the pot. Then picking up a knife she snapped her fingers and the fridge door creaked open. All three approached the open door warily. Holding the knife at a warning angle, Aunt Dot sprang forward, thrust her arm up to the armpit into the depths of the fridge and emerged with a cry of triumph and a pot of margarine. "Right!" she exclaimed. "Now let's try for the bread!"

Later, climbing high on the hills, in warm sunshine and unusually fresh air, the children discussed this approach to food.

"I know it's live yoghurt, but is it *meant* to come when it's called?"

"Dunno. What was that plant with the silvery bits in the leaves?"

"That was a different yoghurt. The silvery bits were the lid."
"You mean it ate its way through a silver foil lid? When it was dead?"

"Re incarnation?"

"Then what had it come back as?"

"Even if you're dead you've got to look lively to survive in that fridge."

"And, we have got bits of it with us..."

"Let's go and sit over there by the pond. I want to talk." Chris pointed at a convenient rock. The two teenagers wandered over the grass towards the tarn, and sat down in the sunshine.

"I wish Dad hadn't sent us away." Linda said, standing up and brushing the stone clean before sitting down again.

"Me too. Aunt Dot's OK, and I like Uncle Ben, but I'd rather be at home."

"There's nothing to do here, and I miss mum."

"Even though all she did was shout at us?"

"Yeah."

"Bet you miss MacDonalds more," Chris slandered her.

"Don't be rotten."

"Linda, did you see what happened in the garden last night?"

"All I saw was two blokes in weird gear, who tried to argue with Auntie Dot and got away with it," Linda answered.

"Uncle hit one of them."

"At least he's not having to hop round going Rivet, Rivet and trying to catch flies."

"Uncle Ben?"

"No, the one he hit on the head."

"Well, then they had an argument, Aunt Dot and Uncle Ben. Uncle thought we might be in danger from the Watches."

"A bad tempered Rolex? A Breitling that's gone to the dark side?"

"No, idiot. I think he meant the blokes in the garden. But Auntie said we should be OK if we didn't know what was going on."

"You've only ever known what was going on when you were eating."

"I thought that was you. Anyway, Uncle said he was going North for a scout round, to look for their gate."

"There's lots of gates round here. Must be a special one."

"What gate? Watergate? Irangate? Lancastergate Services?"

"Dunno. Look, someone's coming."

Walking slowly with a thick staff and a dog at his side a figure climbed easily up the fell. As it came closer, they recognised the youth they had met in the lane yesterday. Gradually, he came closer, before coughing dreadfully, and stopping to light a cigarette. Still coughing, he sat down on the end of the rock. His dog also sat beside him, and eyed the children's rucksack warily.

"Ello..cofcofcofcofcofcofcofcofcof."

"Hi. You're... Ned, right?" asked Chris.

"Yeah. Someone has to be, and I drew the short straw. You two runnin' away then?"

"No. We've just come out for a walk."

"Hard to tell the difference, sometimes."

"What do you want?"

"Just passin'." Ned leant back, nearly fell off the rock and quickly straightened up again.

"What, up here? On the top of a fell, miles from anywhere?"

"Aye, that's why it's called a Pass yer see? Just passin'... People pass. Do yer know the password?"

"What password?"

"The one that lets yer pass, of course."

"But we were only going back to the cottage."

"That's what you think. Grotbags has got something I want, and you're a key to get it for me." He raised his staff, and a cold wind began to blow softly, spreading a chill down the teenagers' spines.

"*Garoth. Nam Garoth.*" A mist formed about the stone. Chris picked up the haversack, and Linda eyed the dog nervously.

"*Garoth, Narbel Garoth.*" The mist began to swirl about them in an alarming fashion. Linda could hear soft voices whispering, and began to look terrified.

"You asked for it!" yelled Chris, and grabbing a yoghurt pot from the bag he hurled it at Ned's feet. The mist made a disturbing sound, and vanished at once. The dog backed off, snarling as the yoghurt pot rocked alarmingly. A set of yellow fronds sprouted from the lid, and waved in a threatening manner.

Ned took a step back. "What in Hades is *that?*" he yelled, as the fronds waved towards him. The pot lurched across the grass, and he stepped back again, hurriedly.

"The password?" asked Chris, innocently, and then he and Linda turned and ran. Ned stepped further back, until his feet were in the water.

"What's eating him?" gasped Chris, as they fled down the hillside.

"Something with a dark and wanton side," Linda panted. "Then it got into Auntie's fridge. God knows what it is now, but I don't want to find out."

Above them on the hill, Ned was joined by his junior wizard, who prodded at the yoghurt with his staff. The yoghurt ate the staff, and the two ran for it, leaving the pot to slowly sink into the tarn leaving a trail of satisfied mauve bubbles. Chris and

Linda ran for the cottage. Behind, they could hear the dog give chase. Closer now came the garden fence… As Uncle Ben opened the door and called urgently to his wife, another cowled figure appeared from behind some trees. He gave a lazy wave of the arm, and the grass around the children's feet sprang alight. Flames burst and roared around them as they crashed through the garden gate, and ran up the path. Their uncle shepherded them through the door without turning his gaze from the three figures, now in black cloaks and cowls that stood at the gate. Uncle Ben stepped back, and closed the door firmly. Linda was crying.

"Who are they, Auntie?"

"They are from Caer Surdin. Quick, Ben get them in the cellar. They look shaken."

"Like a Martini?"

"Is that like a foreign sparrow? Can't be doing with them in the house, droppings all over the cushions."

There was a bang on the door, which shook. The door, that is, not the bang.

"Quick. The cellar. *NOW.*"

"Are we being salted away?"

"Don't go nuts. This is for your own safety."

The cellar door swung open, and the children were given a torch and pushed into the damp, dark space at the top of the cellar steps. As the cellar door swung shut behind them, the cottage door fell in and a weird purple light show took place in the kitchen. Any rich rock band would have salivated at the prospect of having it on their stage. There followed the sound of scratching and dragging. Green and orange light seeped under the cellar door, to illuminate a space that was better left dark. Not because it was evil, or eldritch, but just very dirty. Aunt Dot had long since rid herself of the unnecessary virtue of housework. Out of sight, unclean. The dragging noise stopped, and then a long rising scream of fear and terror rose, and rose… and stopped.

Somehow the silence was worse.

"Chris."

"What, Linda?"

"There's a sign here on the wall."

"What does it say?"

"Pass the torch. Keep the flame."

"But it's an electric torch."

"No, that's the sign."

"Pass the torch?"

"Were you born daft?"

"What does Keep The Flame mean?"

"Dunno. I don't like crosswords. They annoy me."

"You should take these chains and place them round your necks."

"Did you say that, Chris?"

"Say what?"

"You should take these chains and place them round your necks."

"No."

"Good. It was me after all," said the third voice in the dark. "Nearly had me worried, then."

Upstairs came the sound of battle, and then suddenly a plate smashed.

"That's torn it," said the voice.

"How do you tear a plate?"

"She's a bit house proud, your aunt."

"Aunt Dot? The green queen?"

"House proud?"

"Oh yeah, I've often seen her polishing the spiders, bringing in the goat (cheaper than a Dyson), pushing the goat out afterwards. Cleaning up after the goat. Really, it's a microcosm of all human life there. Mostly futile of course, which is why it is such a good metaphor. No real understanding, just a desire to eat. Like the goat. And the fridge."

The silence on the other side of the door took on a quality linked often with frying bacon. A sort of sizzle, which was somehow, a little more scary than the zaps, bangs and squishes. Then, glowing eerily in the darkness, a liquid started to seep under the door into the cellar. It was a rather unpleasant shade of green, with yellow and orange flecks. And some red bits, which seemed to swim around as if alive, and were looking for something. Anything. Even the reader, so take care not to linger here.

"Man, they are *really* getting stuck in there," said the voice in the darkness, with a note of concern now in its tone.

"Look," started Linda.

"At what?" the voice enquired urgently.

Linda stamped her foot, and coughed at the cloud of dust that rose up and covered her.

"Who are you?" she managed, with a burst of racking coughs that would have brought tears of financial gain to the eyes of any private ENT doctor.

"I'm Fungus."

"Is that a name or a description?"

"I'm a BogTroll. I have been stopping here, in this cellar in your aunt's place, and right now I'm sort of planning to save your lives."

At the bottom of the stairs, Chris could make out a faint green glow. Like many cellar dwelling BogTrolls, Fungus had become faintly luminous, to help him see in the dark. Some trolls found their way about by plucking small bits of their bodies (which regenerated) and lobbing the bits around, wandering round by the light of the lump.

Chris sniffed, hard. "Why can I smell mushrooms?"

"Yeah, sorry. Can't grow plants without sunlight, so I make do with mushrooms. *Certain* mushrooms, know what I mean?"

"So why do you live in the cellar?" asked Linda, now eying the green goo oozing slowly in her direction, from the edge of the closed door.

"Mainly, it's the smell. Your aunt doesn't wash all that often, you know. Partly cos she says I have worse table manners than the goat, partly cos of the philosophy, and mainly cos of the jazz."

"The jazz?"

"Well, that's how I got my name. Fungus the Boogieman." The troll pulled a large, and only slightly battered, saxophone out from under a pile of sacks. "Course, I play some rock and blues too. Comes of being a rolling stone."

"A Rolling Stone? The band?"

"No, I've just got a bit of a weight problem."

"Linda," Chris hissed urgently, "this stuff is getting closer."

"UGH!!!!!"

"Yeah," called Fungus, moving quickly to the bottom of the steps. "Get down here quick, cos if that stuff is what I think it is, then it eats most things. Including wooden stairs."

Quickly, but cautiously, the children moved towards the green glow at the bottom of the stairs. Getting closer, they could see a roughly man sized shape (rather overweight) with a pair of dark glasses and a baseball cap with the legend **FRODO LIVES** He seemed to be smiling, but it was probably hard to tell.

"What do you think is happening up there?" asked Linda.

"Well," said Fungus, "she could be entertaining visitors. It's more likely that she's upset with someone. Were you followed into the house?"

"Yes."

"Well, the Council Environmental Health is a strong possibility."

These came a violent bang, followed by a howl of triumph, a heavy bang on the ceiling, and the sound of Aunt Dot swearing in Urdu (or possibly Yorkshire, it was hard to tell).

"On the other hand," remarked Fungus, lazily stepping aside to avoid a heavy lamp falling from the ceiling into his previously occupied personal space, "maybe not.

Sounds like someone threw something heavy. Hope it wasn't yer aunt. Must be a professional dispute."

Chris and Linda looked at each other.

"Politicians throw votes – and abuse – at each other. The magically inclined throw other things. Cauldrons, curries, goats, or spells to turn each other into one of the above."

"What, turn each other into politicians? Isn't that a bit nasty?" asked Chris.

"Solicitors would be worse."

"Will they be all right?" asked Linda, eyeing the green goo, which was now slowly coming down the stairs leaving aged, oak wood behind it, and making happy burbling noises as it came.

"Don't fret." Fungus tried to reassure her, as all three backed away, Fungus pausing to grab the sacking he used to wrap around his sax. "Most of the bigwigs of each side are off holding conventions in France. This lot should just make a nasty mess, can't be worse than when the dips got spilt at yer aunt's last party."

"I'm having trouble believing this," complained Chris.

"Then try believing we already escaped. It might work, and save me from some heavy exercise." With a crash, the stairs folded up into the goo, which burped hugely, and continued to spread across the cellar floor. Oak aged goo?

"Well," said Fungus, "I'm gonna split. Coming?" He grunted as he bent over, and pulling more sacks aside, revealed a large trapdoor which, not without some effort and a lot of swearing, (which has been deleted from the narrative on decency grounds) he pulled open. "Come and meet some dwarfs. I know that they are vertically challenged (short) folliclly challenged (hairy) and spatially challenged (fat) but its better than staying here and being drunk."

"We are too young to get drunk."

"*Being* drunk. By that Green stuff."

"I'm with you," said Chris quickly.

"Are dwarfs chronically challenged too?" giggled Linda nervously.

"No. They just seem to live for bloody ever."

A loud, happy noise told all three that the green goo had found

Fungus' mushrooms. Fungus promptly jumped down into the hole, and the two children (with a backwards glance at the goo, once green but now flashing with all the colours of the rainbow) followed him. The drop was about five feet, and with unaccustomed chivalry Chris managed not to land on his sister, who had gone first. In the joint light of the faintly glowing BogTroll and the torch, they could see a tunnel, clearly well made and level floored, but extremely dark, heading off into the distance. The goo advanced to the edge of the hole. "You wouldn't get *me* down there," it muttered, and turned back to graze on the rest of the mushrooms. The children followed Fungus the Boogieman down the long dark passage into the earth.

CHAPTER THREE

On the morning after the night before, it rained. Grizelda found this an enormous help – for a start, it encouraged the goat to come into the kitchen and help clear up. Secondly, it discouraged the fridge from going outside. On its own. The magical battle had been fought to a no score draw, with the Watches making a hurried strategic withdrawal to previously prepared positions (or in non-technical language, running away). Since then, the fridge had rather evolved. Always inclined to behave as it liked, except for the tempo – spatial reality plane, (which for the linguistically challenged means it had tended to stay where it was put, when it was put there) the fridge had now taken to moving around the kitchen of its own accord, occasionally opening its door in a menacing way.

The fact that all the contents had overnight changed into either Greek yoghurt or liver pate did not, on the whole, reassure the casual observer that its intentions were pacifistic. The kitchen based element of the green goo had been chivvied, mopped and finally threatened with the goat until it had been corralled into a large bucket in the corner, where it gave off a greasy aroma, occasional burps and demands for mushrooms. Broken plates had been put in the bin, and Uncle Ben was washing down the walls. Occasionally, he looked round to try and find out what was making a scraping sound behind him, in case it was the fridge.

"You know," Ben remarked thoughtfully, "we really should let the kids out now, Grizelda."

"Oh blast! Quiet forgot them."

"Quite forgot?"

"No. They were being quiet, so I forgot them." She took off her black, pointed hat and unlocked the cellar door. "Come out you two, it's Aunt Dot. Come on, it's safe now, and we could use some help with the goat."

There was no reply.

"Chris? Linda? Hello? Ben, they seem not to be there."

"Wasn't Fungus visiting? He won't have eaten them. Will he?"

"You're right. You're wrong."

"Can't you tell the difference yet? I mean, I know that yer a witch and all that…"

"Don't be more stupid than yer have to be, do you know how much you sounded like my bank manager?" retorted Grizelda.

"Insults will get you nowhere." Ben stared into the cellar "It's a bit dark."

"Then turn the light on!" Grizelda peered over his shoulder into the dark cellar.

"Come on, Dot. We switched the power off to try and deal with the fridge, remember?"

"Maybe Fungus took the bulb out."

"Nah, he needed that for the mushrooms."

There was a scraping noise behind her, then with a yell Grizelda bumped hard into Ben, and together they fell down the remains of the steps.

Some scientists have carried out experiments into gravity. One method was to take two objects of different sizes, say an elephant and a mouse, up a tall tower, and encourage them to jump to see how long it took for them to land. The elephant was chosen as being large and self-propelled, and the mouse was chosen as the elephant's self-propeller. (Plus it was easier to lob over the balcony after the elephant had gone.)

Anyway, the reason for the experiments was two fold. Firstly the experimenters needed some first class fertiliser, obtained from the elephant, and secondly to measure the relative velocity of each animal. After a while however, they reached the conclusion that the continuous fall of elephants was

- A   reducing the supply
- B   damaging the foundations, hence
- C   causing the tower to lean, thereby
- D   distorting the statistical results, as
- E   it was obvious that the heaviest would land first

The occasional animal rights protest group had been a nuisance, but usually dealt with by encouraging them to try and catch the elephant as it landed. Although she had not read of the results, Grizelda ensured that when she and Ben replicated the experiment, she landed second. On top. Even gravity can be overcome by positive thinking.

"Why did yer have to do that?" groaned Ben, picking Grizelda off his chest, and trying to stand up.

"Not me. It were the fridge."

"The fridge never had a grip like that."

"*It spoke to me.*"

"What did it say?" asked Ben, backing away slightly.

"Chill out."

"You've been spending too much time with Fungus. Do yer think it's safe to go back up there yet?"

"Give it ten minutes, Ben. Where are the kids?"

"Don't think they can be here. The row we made falling, they would have come to see what was going on."

Aunt Dot pulled back her sleeve, raised a hand, and a fireball rose slowly towards the ceiling.

"Which Fireball spell's that one then?"

"XL 5* of course. Not here, are they. Fungus must have taken them off."

[* One for the older reader there.]

"They went that way", said the heap of green goo sleepily from a corner, where it was contemplating its navel and the meaning of life (I eat to live. Therefore I am what I ate. Ergo, I am a mushroom. Isn't logic wonderful?)

"The secret passage!"

"Didn't know we had one" said Ben, dubiously.

"That's because it's a secret. Goes to the Helvyndelve, by the Old Gate at the Bowderstone."

"But how would they get in?" Ben wondered. Then he swung round, and stared in the fading glow at a patch of wall that was conspicuously empty. "They have taken the Wards of Lingard!"

"Good. Dwarfs will let them in then. Be safe there, till we go an' get them. Now let's see if the fridge will let us get back into the kitchen, I could murder some toast."

"With pate?"

"You might regret that remark."

Far, far down in the dark tunnel, the children huddled together in terror. Fungus was singing. "You can do anything, but lay off of me Blue Swede Shoes!!!!!"

As the terrible echoes faded, Linda ventured, "Fungus, shouldn't that be blue suede shoes?"

"I learnt it from a Viking. Fancy a mushroom?" Fungus pulled his sax from the sacks and reflectively started to play Wild Thing for his private amusement. The awful echoes ran round and ahead of them, possibly to get away, until a small section of the tunnel wall collapsed. "Wow, man! The power of music!" exclaimed the wild saxcavator.

Out of the hole appeared a small, bearded helmet." Can't you keep it down? It's not easy singing acapella in a mine anyway, and with that noise it's near impossible." The whole dwarf came out of the hole.

"Hi Lakin," said Fungus, cheerfully. "Meet my buddies, if I can remember their names, er…"

"Chris," said Chris.

"Linda," said Linda.

"Humans," said Lakin, mournfully. "Don't like humans. Except in stew of course. What do they want, Fungus?"

The troll drew himself up to his full height and declaimed: "Sanctuary from the myrmidididididididiions of Caer Surdin, oh Lord!" The effect was somewhat spoiled by the lump of mud that fell from the roof of the tunnel onto his head at that point.

Lakin looked at him. "You off your trolley? Listen, Fungus, you need to lay off the mushrooms a bit, know what I mean?"

"No, honest. We've just come down from Grotbags' pad, and the Watches were having themselves a real time there. You should have seen the colours!"

"Probably would have reminded me of that time you were sick in Frank's bar."

"Excuse me," said Linda, "but are dwarfs supposed to talk like that?"

"You come down a dark passage, following a luminous troll who is wearing Ray Bans and a stupid cap, and you wish to criticise my syntax?"

"I can see his point," muttered Chris.

"No you can't!" retorted Lakin, but adjusted his chain mail anyway.

"Look, be cool and let us in," urged Fungus. "Before half Caer Surdin follows us down this tunnel!"

"Are you saying you were serious?"

"Was Elvis cool?"

"Not if he was cremated."

"Everyone," remarked Fungus huffily, "knows that he was kidnapped by aliens. Now, what about letting us in? These kids are in the care of Grizelda of the Fourth Pentangle."

"What, these are Grotbag's kids? We've heard of them. Do you know what they did to that Ned earlier today?"

"Didn't do nothing to him!" said Chris, angrily.

"I heard you threatened him. With a yoghurt. From the Fridge."

They all shuddered. Fungus treated them to a cold stare. "Just tell me you are not tooled up with any more of those live yoghurts."

Linda looked in her bag. "No. But the pots were all dead yoghurt, it said so on the side."

"Then why do they keep moving about? Still, If Surdin is after you, I suppose we should keep you safe, eh Lakin?"

The dwarf grunted in a surly fashion, and pulled down a little more of the wall, to climb back into his tunnel.

"What's through there?" asked Linda.

"The Helvyndelve," said Fungus.

Lakin struck a dramatic pose, spoiled only by his stepping on his own beard and staggering sideways into the wall as he missed the whole hole. "The Ancient Halls of the Dwarf Kingdom," he declaimed.

"Bit like a Theme Park, really," whispered Fungus. "It's all just show, and secretly the staff all hate you."

"Please, Fungus," asked Linda, "what is Caer Surdin?"

"Well," Fungus said sitting down on a bit of spoil from the hole Lakin had made in the wall, and so spoiling the effect of the hole in the wall: "there's sort of a low level war going on."

"*A War!*"

"Goodies and baddies?" asked Chris.

"Well, sort of baddies, that's your aunt et al -"

("Who is Al?" Lakin asked Fungus, only to receive a glare)

"and" continued Fungus, "worsies. Didn't yer aunt tell you?"

"She doesn't tell us anything."

"She told us to get in the cellar," admitted Linda.

"I don't think that counts," remarked Lakin, with a sneer. "Still, you'd better come inside. And you, Fungus, one bloody HIHO and you're for it."

"Yeah, yeah. Keep yer beard on."

"It's not detachable you know."

"Yo, Lakin! What's goin' down?" called a new voice from the hole in the tunnel wall, and another dwarf head came into sight. "Hey, Fungus! We playing then, or what?"

"Haemar, meet some friends of mine." Fungus grinned. "Kids, this is Haemar, he's cool."

Chris and Linda looked closely at the dwarf, whose helmet seemed odd – then they realised that it had pictures etched into the metal. Linda looked carefully at one of the pictures, and promptly wished she hadn't.

"Hey kids, any friend of Fungus." Haemar's voice dropped. "Listen, Fungus, got some good stuff here. Got it from the guy who runs the second hand rune store on the 14th Level. Brewed it himself. You fancy it, there's some mates comin' over tonight. Lose Lakin and the kids, and bring the sax and we'll jam."

"Sounds cool to me." hissed back Fungus. "Right," he said normally, or as close to normal as a luminous green troll can manage, "let's get down."

"Fungus," said Chris, "we are underground already. What can be down?"

"Down, deeper and down of course. No, you are too young to know that one. The Helvyndelve is down." Fungus stomped off after the dwarfs, who were loading tools and short swords onto metal-framed backpacks.

"What happens if they get near a magnet?" Linda asked Fungus.

Haemar overheard her. "Happened to Fundun once. Took us

four days to stop him walking round in circles. Mind you, the cooks found him useful – gave him a spoon and used him to stir the stew."

Lakin shuddered at the memory. "Tasted horrible too," he recalled.

"Yeah. Should have made him walk round on the outside of the pot instead."

The dwarfs set off down the tunnel, and the children, left with few options – none of which they found all that attractive, followed. The tunnel became smooth floored, and slowly rose in height. Graffiti could be seen scrawled on the sidewalls.

"Just like home," muttered Chris. "Dark, smelly, and full of weirdos who write on the walls."

"At least we haven't been mugged yet."

"Wait until you meet the Doorkeepers," said Haemar, who wasn't walking as quickly as the other dwarfs and so had overheard them. "Used to be really cool here, you know? Great parties, the tunnels were clean, it were quiet and peaceful, at least until the parties started, and again after they ended of course, no one laid any heavy worries on each other. But then it all went wrong when the Lord of Helvyndelve went missing with the Amulet of Kings. Things fell apart a bit. Quite a lot of the dwarfs split, some took straight jobs, wound up having to work for a livin'. Sometimes hard to tell them from humans now. Except for the size, of course."

"What do they do?" asked Linda.

"Council, mostly, where they can skive off like the rest. Could be worse."

"What could be worse?"

"DSS?"

They rounded a bend in the tunnel, which opened out into a large airy space. Other tunnels opened into the cavern from other directions. At the end of the cavern were two imposing doors, picked out in patchy gold leaf, with worn inscriptions upon them. The inscriptions were so faded as to be nearly illegible, which was just as well since they told unwelcome visitors to get lost in fourteen languages. A huge pile of cigarette ends lay to one side, in mute testimony to the exciting duties enjoyed by the guards. Slowly, the party approached the Great Doors of Helvyndelve.

"Halt!" commanded a hidden voice. "Who goes there? In the name of the Lord of Helvyndelve (Wherever he's got to, oh rats, what's the next bit Fundun?)…"

Linda and Chris looked at each other. Had they really walked down a long underground tunnel to see rather impressive doors, just to listen to a fourth grade music hall turn?

"Right! Got it, written on back of me shield. What's that word? Right. Declare yerselves, Friends or Foes?"

"What is this?" Chris asked a bored looking Fungus.

"Sort of an entry ritual. Every time anyone approaches the Doors, they go through this."

"Does it make a difference?"

"Nope. Still can't get in without bribing them Actually, that's supposed to be one reason the last Lord went missing. Nipped out without his wallet for a peaceful smoke and this lot wouldn't let him in again. Never been seen since."

"What was the Lord's name?"

"Lucan."

Lakin walked purposefully towards the Doors, and kicked one hard. After hopping on one leg for a moment, cursing, he booted it again. The Door slowly swung open, and a short (sorry, seriously vertically challenged) dwarf peered out. Lakin's arm shot out, grabbing a handful of the beard which was wrapped three times round the guard's waist, and as the dwarf fell off balance Lakin booted him harder than he had kicked the door.

"What's he doing?" hissed Linda to Haemar.

"Negotiating. See, Lakin is the Heir to the Lord, and refuses to pay the entry tolls."

"Should have got entry trolls instead," said Fungus. "He'd have to pay up then."

"Tolls?" asked Chris.

"Told you it was like a theme park," Fungus replied.

"See Linda. It is like home. This is where you can be mugged."

"I wish we were at home now. Why did mum have to go to Leeds, and end up in hospital?"

"Dunno. But this is better than going to a burger bar."

42

Lakin bopped the second guard on the head with his hammer, leaving a ringing tone in the air and a cacophony inside the hit helmet. "Formalities over," he announced. "Welcome to the hallowed halls of the Helvyndelve."

CHAPTER FOUR.

Meanwhile, back at the farmhouse, Aunt Dot and Uncle Ben had managed to get safely out of the cellar, and back into the kitchen. They had been joined by a mysterious figure in a black hooded cloak that hid his face completely and was therefore no bad thing. Aunt Dot fussed about in a noisy sulk. She was concerned about the missing teenagers.

"Why won't you do what I want, and go an' get them!" she demanded.

Uncle Ben puffed a huge cloud of smoke out of his pipe, and tried to hide inside the fumes.

"Becoz," said he in the hood, in a thick accent – that is he sounded strange, not stupid – "I haf better thingz to do. Ned must be found, and otherz are abroad."

"Don't rub it in. We all know I didn't make the conference this year."

"No, I mean otherz are out on the fellz."

"Better," agreed Ben. "Round here they think Yorkshire is foreign."

"Doesn't everyone?"

"Look Erald," carried on Grizelda. "I just don't trust them dwarfs. All that living underground, no natural light, it's just not healthy. And all those underground parties. Not surprising that they don't know when to call it a day, is it?"

"Dinna Ken" said the other, sounding Scottish for a moment.

"Who's Ken?" asked Grizelda, feeling suspicious.

"Whose dinner?" asked Ben, feeling peckish.

"Vait!" commanded Erald. He put the end of his staff to his ear. "Vy they cannot make a headset, Bluetooth vould be good," he grumbled, and then went quiet.

"Vat, I mean what news?" asked Dot, as Erald removed the staff from his ear and cleaned the wax off the end with his cloak.

"Badnewz."

"Bless you," said Ben.

"Nasty cold, that," agreed Grizelda.

"I got vet last week. I have bad newz. My brother he send wordz. Ned has been to Caer Surdin's Gate Between Worlds, and returned with a hozt of Bodgandor, evil goblins. He haz attacked the Edern near Carnedd Llewellyn, making war when our strength is away. Rouze ze dwarfs! Ve must fight. Ze Tuatha will ride against them!"

He stood on the chair, and picked fluff and goat hair off his cloak. It is hard to make am impressive exit when covered in goat hair. "Can you not be cleaning up before I return?" With a flash of golden light, he vanished, leaving wisps of smoke in the air and charred flecks on the floor.

"Every time he does that, me pipe goes out," complained an unimpressed Ben.

"You know he's a member of the Clean Air Campaign."

"Then why does he always smell like that?"

"It's a personal problem Have a bit of charity."

"She won't let me," joked her husband.

Flourishing her mop, his wife glared at him. "Don't let me catch you with that witch!"

"Don't be jealous. You know that you are bigger and nastier than she is."

"Flattery? Do you know what me mother said about men who flattered?"

"Your mother? She flattened men, not got flattered by them. It were because of yer mother that we had that plague of frogs in the village, and half the girls had to go to Kendal to find blokes instead."

"Yeah," reminisced Dot, smiling. "She loved using that frog spell. Shame she's not here now."

"Not really. Seeing as we cremated her."

"We could have put her in a pot. Kept her on the mantelpiece."

"And have her rattle the lid every time I lit up? And can you image what she'd have done to the goat?"

"Um. Mind you, she'd have kept the fridge in order."

"Now I'm more concerned about keeping Bodgandor in order. It's been a while sin anyone round here got hold of them. Ned's getting good, or uppity. Or both."

"Must be that new suit he got through mail order. I knew we'd have trouble when he went in for power dressing."

"I thought that was something you put on salad."

Grizelda glared at him. She put nothing on salad, even insisting on removing the slugs before eating.

"Bodgandor. Hum. There's not as many as there used to be, thank the Gods. And the Edern? Why should they be fighting here? Haven't they enough trouble with their investment banking business? Since they got short of cash, half the dwarfs in their patch have left and they have trouble maintaining enough juice to run that Fairy Hill of theirs. Temporal abnormalities need lots of power."

"I thought they had wind generators?"

"Town and Country planning closed them down   I tell you, the magic's goin out of life."

"What about the kids?" Grizelda was still relatively worried.

"Erald was right. They're better off in Helvyndelve right now, if it's goin to get rough. They will be as safe as can be, unless we send them home."

"To Manchester? Suppose a small war would be safer than that, and they might be a help."

"Well, I'm told it's a bit mucky in Helvyndelve these days, what with the cleaners walking out. They'll have plenty to do."

"Cleaning up?"

"Nah, kicking over the full rubbish bins."

At this point there came a huge crash, and lime green smoke billowed in under the door from the study. A further explosion took the study door off its hinges, and the lights went out.

"Cor!" came an amazed voice from the darkness. "It worked! Page 15, spell 27B. It only worked! HOT DAM!"

"Sorry," retorted Ben. "You've made her a bit frosty instead."

"Have you any idea," snarled Grizelda, with ice in her tones, "how much a joiner is going to charge to fix that?"

"Err," was the incisive reply. One of the Watches emerged from the swirling dust and goat hair into the kitchen, carrying a short sword, which was still dripping spots of green light onto the floor. Grizelda was not amused, and it showed.

"You can have the cleaning bill this time. And what do yer mean, bustin' in at this time of night? Can't the war wait until business hours? Do yer know how much money yer losing by not driving the late night pub trade home?"

The apprentice to evil hesitated at that, and turned back to look into the darkness behind him." She's got a point there. Do me expenses include loss of earnings, cos its good money this time of night?"

"Silence!" hissed Ned, emerging from the darkness and using a menacing tone, probably learnt from watching too many reruns of The Godfather. "This evening, we are abroad..."

"No we're not. We're not even in Yorkshire," objected Ben.

"About then," sniffed Ned, struggling to keep the heavy menace going in the face of dreadful provocation: "on an errand of evil intent, to visit terror an dread on the citizenry."

"Just another TV talent show, then," sneered Ben. "I'd go for overtime too, if I were you, mate."

"SHUT UP, can't yer!"

Grizelda turned to Ben. "It's Ned," she said in surprise. "Last time he were here, the rake got him."

"This time, its different," said Ned sulkily, not liking the reminder. His assistant did not like the reminder either.

"Lets just pay for the door and go," he advised. Ned brushed him aside, and the apprentice fell into a large pile of assorted goat hair and rat droppings, which Dot had been planning to turn into a muffler for the last two years. Muffled sneezes rose from the pile, which twitched spasmodically. At least Grizelda's plan had worked in a way.

"There's things in here with me," complained the pile in hushed tones.

"Hush!" exclaimed Ned. "Grizelda, prepare your soul to do battle with utmost evil."

"I thought that was you," Ben said to his wife.

"Flatterer."

"Prepare to meet – a Taxman!" declaimed Ned.

"At least its not DSS."

Ned stepped to one side, sneering. From behind him loomed a tall, bent figure, faintly outlined in red. It had four arms, each carried an object of terrible menace: a calculator, pen, briefcase, and all five official volumes of the Taxes Acts – the ones in official bindings, which even terrify accountants.

"Heavens!" gasped Ben. "He meant it, do something, Dot."

Grizelda swallowed. "Didn't think he had it in him."

Looming before them, the ghastly figure waved a hand, and in a blaze of red light conjured a desk and three chairs. The only comfy chair was behind the desk, and the Taxman took it. Relishing the thought of its prey, it placed the weapons of Mad Destruction on the desk, and peered at them from behind its half moon spectacles.

"My name is Jeremy," it announced. All in the room shuddered. This was worse than they had imagined.

Grizelda took a deep breath, and screamed defiance. "Begone, Foul Shade of Night, and trouble us no more, that walk living beneath the moon!"

"Nah," dismissed the Taxman. "Might work on Incapacity Benefit Agents, but no chance with me." One hand scratched its nose, a second scratched what they hoped was its bum, and the third carefully selected a volume from the table. "I shall now read to you each article and sub clause of the Taxes Management Act 1970 (as amended), with the commentaries from the last two budget statements, and the associated Inland Revenue press releases at the time."

"What's them?" hissed Ben. Predictably, Ned knew. "That's where they hide all the really nasty bits that they don't want to admit to in public."

"Ta. I always wanted to know that."

"Don't mention it."

"Won't then."

"Suit yerself."

"I've got an idea," whispered Grizelda. She stood up and walked into the privy. The taxman never looked up, as he carefully located the first chosen passage, without needing to look at the index.

"There's no escape," called Ned. "The place is surrounded."

"I don't think she were thinking of that," answered Ben. "I suppose that this evil doom were your idea, then Ned?"

"Oh yes, and I'm looking forward to it. Got some new earmuffs an all, so that I won't have to hear a word. Or the screaming."

As Grizelda walked back into the room, a telephone started ringing. It had that particularly annoying ringtone with which some phones are equipped as standard, designed to irritate everyone but the owner.

"That's odd," said Ben.

"Why?"

"We haven't got a mobile phone."

The Taxman glared, and opened his briefcase, pulled out a mobile phone and put it to his only functioning ear. "I'm in the middle of an interview here. What? The Regional Controller? Promotion? I'm on the way." It stood up and rapidly packed all the papers back into its case. "Don't think that you are off the hook," it snarled. "Your cards are marked, but I've got better fish to fry at the moment." The taxman waved an arm, and the taxman, desk and all the chairs vanished, leaving a red glow and a faint smell of haddock.

Grizelda smiled, nastily, from her new seat on the floor. "I think he's been trawled."

Ned backed off, and ran through the door into the kitchen, shutting the door behind him. Ben and Grizelda looked at each other.

"Bad move," said Ben. There came the sound of scraping, then a wild cry of terror and running feet which dopplered away into the distance.

Cautiously, they opened the kitchen door and peered into the kitchen. The fridge stood quiet, its door gaping. "Cunning!" said Ben admiringly. "Switched it to defrost when it went for him, and did a runner. Wish I'd thought of that."

The fridge gave him a hurt look, and scraped back to its place near the back door. A thin trickle of liquid seeped under its door, and began to etch the stone flags.

The sea mist crept in from the sea (where else did you think?) and crawled across the hills. The forlorn cry of a lonely seagull echoed eerily across the bare rocks.

Dimly in the mist loomed a standing stone. Well, being stone it just stood there, of course, not being capable of your actual movement. It is more mystical to say it loomed. It could lurk instead, if you really prefer – the stone was not too bothered either way. Just getting by on this mist haunted cliff top was hard enough.

Through the mist, from opposite directions, came four cloaked and booted figures. They loomed rather better than the stone. One was dressed in black, the others in grey, which made them hard to see. They nodded, without speaking, and waited. Beside the stone grew, slowly, a circle of brilliant light. The light grew brighter and brighter, the circle became an orb, which crackled with lightning, until a fifth member joined the group. "Do we always have to meet in the middle of nowhere? In the rain?" Two more shining orbs appeared, disgorging two more sets of cloaks and boots. Sort of an eldritch M&S? Both the newcomers carried spears, and one had a guitar on his back as well. Otherwise, it was impossible to tell any of them apart.

"The Stone of Lath," said Finn, the last to arrive.

"Look we know where we are, or we wouldn't have got here," said Liamm, the second to arrive.

"Uh?" asked Diarmid.

"You know what I mean. Can't we get on with it? I was in the middle of bridge, and halfway to a small slam."

"Would you like a Grand Slam, with this staff?"

"Not unless it's got the Ace of Spades up its sleeve."

Brother Tuatha," cried Erald, who had been first to arrive and was fed up with getting wet, "long has it been since we met at The Stone of Lath." His strange accent had gone, obviously just put on earlier for effect.

"Can anyone remember how far it is to the pub?"

"Yeah, we'd started meeting in the Rose an Crown down in the valley. Nice barmaid, too."

"They have a good folk night on Tuesdays."

"Is there a good night for folk?"

"Yes. Any night when I'm not there."

"Quiet! Surdin moves."

"Wish we could, me feet are bloody freezing."

"And it's only half an hour to closing."

"And it's not Tuesday."

"We, the Tuatha, are met to ask the Edern to ride with us against the new strength gathered by the evil wizards of Caer Surdin," announced Erald.

"Not sure about that," moaned Diarmid. "They keep on singing those old songs no one understands, and complain when I get me guitar out."

"We all complain when you get that out."

One of the black cloaked Tuatha looked furtively round and the grey clad Edern, and muttered: "they are as bad as that blasted Dago, too. Every time they see a windmill, they yell Charge!"

"Windmillophobia. Well-known, wossname, phobia that is. Catch it in Spain a lot."

"Phobia? You mean it's all in their minds?"

"Can you charge the windmills of your mind?" asked Finn.

"Bet you the Gas supplier would have a go. Charge for anything they can."

"Look," said Erald, trying to take charge again, "we need their help."

"Their help? Load of fairies?"

"They shorten the odds."
"On account of only being four and a half foot high?"

"On account of there being a lot of them."

"If it's only numbers," suggested Finn who disliked the Edern after taking some investment advice from them and losing a lot of money, "there's this guy I know down the pub with a lot of mates."

"Is he any good with a sword?"

"Dunno, but he's pretty nifty with the arrows."

"Longbow? Crossbow?"

"Darts, mostly."

"Fantastic. A damn great evil goblin army comes sweeping across the hillside, and we can stop them by saying: no further until you throw a treble twenty?"

"No need to be like that. I was only trying to help," sulked Finn.

"Come on, first crisis we face in Aeons, and we argue."

"What's Ian got to do with it?"

"He's got the Rose and Crown."

"Can you have a crisis in the pub, if you are a landlord?" Finn asked Diarmid.

"Course you can, if you run out of ale."

"Aye, a terrible thing is a pub with no beer."

"SHUT UP," yelled Erald. "I don't give two hoots what Aeon, no, Ian, does when he runs out of beer. I do care about a herd of Bodgandor loose!"

"Me too!" cut in Diarmid. They all stared at him. "Well, they all drink lager, don't they? Can't stand lager. Drinkers are all louts."

"What about the Edern?" asked Finn.

"Think they are on shorts, what with being small."

They all tried to ignore him.

"EdernLords!" called Erald. The grey clad shapes drifter closer. They made no sound on the wet turf, and shimmered in the mist.

"Hail," announced their leader, Telem.

"Isn't the rain bad enough?" shivered Finn.

"Lord Telem," Erald called. "We ride against the horde of Bodgandor and ask that your folk ride with us."

"Why is he always so pompous?" asked Finn.

"Dunno, think he's got a geas," replied Diarmid.

"What, a big flappy bird with a bad attitude?"

"Something like that yeah."

"Sounds like the barmaid at the Rose and Crown to me."

"A geas wouldn't make me pompous. Fond of roast geas mebbe."

Diarmid looked at his brother, and found he was lost for words, something he had not experienced since contracting laryngitis. Erald ignored them both. He found it easiest in the long run.

Lord Telem was considering Erald's plea. "Bodgandor, loose on the countryside, will only harm us all," he announced. "I feel sure that if I were in a position to consult with the full board…"

"I'm bored already," muttered Finn.

"Then," Telem continued, "the Management would pass an immediate resolution in favour of palliative efforts to ensure that disconcerting, depreciatory, denigatory and unprofitable actions are met with swift, decisive censorious bellicosity."

Finn turned to Diarmid. "What?"

"I think he said yes."

"Let there be no confusion, no laxity in expression or failure through diversity of approach!" announced Telem.

"What?"

"Yes, with knobs on, I think."

Lord Telem beckoned to one of his colleagues, who drifter closer to take instructions.

"We shall muster in the Land of Sinadon. Home of the Lakes," he ordered, and the underling moved off, pulled a mobile phone from his pocket and started muttering in to it urgently.

"How long, Lord Telem, will the muster take?" asked Erald, politely.

"Hum. Currency's a bit flat at the moment, and so a couple of the departments had to move into commodities, futures need to be consolidated for a downtime of a couple of days against marked speculations, so in three days we can be ready to join battle."

"Three days!" exclaimed Erald, shocked.

"Well, the auditors would give the Board a very hard time if we undertook a major operation without detailed preplanning and the installation of safeguards against unforeseen market movements. Then we need to arrange proper emergency cover. Can't just drop everything, old chap. Half the country's banks would end up in Chaos!"

"Who'd notice the difference?" asked Diarmid, sourly.

"We, and our host will be ready to fight at Bed Brannwyn, in three nights from now."

"Thank you, Lord Telem," said Erald formally.

The mist haunted figures moved slowly out of sight, with arcane phrases drifting back. "Shame what happened to the ERN."

"Ya, just have to trust the Government to muck it up on their own now."

"Finn, what's an Edern ERN?"*

"Too bloody much, by the sound of it. Bunch of Bankers."

[* Just can't beat the old jokes.]

*

Three days later, high in the mountains, two figures could be seen by the passing wildlife. To maintain narrative continuity and assist small businesses in the niche-clothing sector, both were robed in black. The local outfitters for witches, warlocks and wizards were with Henry Ford on consumer marketing: any colour you like, so long as it is black. The rain fell heavily. It had had plenty of practice, and was getting good at its job now.

"Did yer order rain, Boss?"

"No, Ned. It's the weather."

"Great effect. Where did it learn to do that?"

The leader of the Evil Ones looked wearily at his chosen assistant, and sighed. "Come," he said, "exercise your responsibility."

"You want me to go jogging with yer, Boss?"

Dimly below them in the valley, a double line of horsemen could be seen in the low cloud and mist. The sound of a horn rang out. "Look!" said the older man, as the dark horde of Bodgandor emerged from the rocks and flung themselves at the horsemen, who turned, formed a line and drove at their foe. The attackers broke, and fled amongst the rocks. The line of Edern reformed, and rode on.

"Our troops are at the valley end, and many Edern will be lost before they reach Talybolyon."

"Do they not have a map?"

"No, Ned, lost to our forces. Now I have a task worthy of your training. I wish you to penetrate the Helvyndelve, and seek to recover the Amulet that the stupid dwarfs have lost. Here is a silver compass which reacts to the power of strong magic, and will help lead you to the Amulet once you are inside the vast halls below us. Once we have it in our power, the whole world will be alight, as one candle in the darkness."

"Hey, that's *really* nasty. Broadcast Barry Manilow records all day long. No one will withstand that."

"Now, be away, and see that you do not fail. Or else, you will wish you had never been born."

Ned bowed, and moved off.

"If he thought more clearly, he would wish I had not been born. Still, who wants a genius as second in command?"

Mist hung in the damp air, and speckled the grass around the horses' hooves as the Edern rode wearily through the valley. Their journey had been hard, and they had been ambushed twice, and had to fight. Their wounded were in the centre of the group, working out insurance claims, and some talked to injury compensation lawyers on their mobiles. Past the end of the lake they rode, and still they were safe from further attack. The valley opened out, and their leader picked up the pace. Then in front of them, strung out across their route to safety, as fearsome as impoverished auditors, rose a swarm of Bodgandor. The leader raised his hand, and signalled a change in formation, they would attack, and those who broke through would survive to meet the muster at Talybolyon. The rest would be mourned by internal memo. The Edern raised their spears:

But now a loud note rang in the air, from no obvious source, as no sensible orchestra leader [an oxymoron there] would take his brass section for early morning practice in the middle of nowhere. Good idea as that undoubtedly is. Annoyed by the harsh tone, the air seemed to split apart as four horsemen, yes in the now obligatory black robes, rode through a light filled archway, which faded behind them, leaving brilliant flecks of golden light to fade in the empty air. As one, they set their spears in rest and charged the Bodgandor, who dropped their various swords, shields etc, and had it away on their toes as fast as they could.

"Oi!" called Diarmid, as the Bodgandor vanished into the mist, "me brother in law could get you some replacements wholesale…"

"Wow," said Finn, looking up at a shape on the nearby hills. "That Ned keeps jumping up and down on his spot."

"Be easier to squeeze it, surely."

"I've still got a headache, travelling about like that," complained Liamm. They all ignored him. Erald rode back to where the Edern sat on their horses, the converse being too uncomfortable.

"Lord Blear."

"Erald, you came in time to be of service to us. Is it in your mission statement?"

"Lord, it was nothing."

"Was it? OK then see you later at the Board Meeting."

"The war council?"

"Yes. We sit at a board."

"And get bored," came a sotto voice remark.

"Could eat a boar."

"Erald can be a bore. Eat him"

"Nah, too bony."

Blear raised his spear, and the company of Edern rode off.

"Is that the one they call Blear?"

"Yes, always got an odd look in his eye."

Liamm looked around the battle arena, with a professional eye. "I wonder how much the garden centre would give us for all this horse muck?"

CHAPTER FIVE

"This passage leads South, then East," said Lakin, as they left the entrance hall.

Chris looked back at the Border Guards getting to their feet, slowly. "Does he always treat Customs like that?"

"Just his custom," replied Haemar. "Bit of a habit, I suppose."

"I think he was trying out, ah, Public relativities" said a further dwarf (called Dain if you were curious. His name was still Dain if you were not, of course.)

"Don't you mean relations?"

"No, he never gets lucky these days."

"See, he's a bit miffed Lucan vanished, losing the Amulet, so he can't have it."

"What does it do?" asked Linda, pretending interest.

"Pretty mean piece of kit. If, wearing it, you sit on the Throne in the Throne Room, you can see almost anything, anywhere, operate all the doings in Helvyndelve, oh and close the Gates between the Worlds that let Caer Surdin bring in the Bodgandor. So when the wearer sits on the Throne of The Mountain King, he can do nearly anything he wants."

"Like a VAT inspector, then?" asked Chris.

"AAAAAAAAARRRRRRRGGGGGHHHHHHHHHH!" screamed a nearby dwarf, pulling out and brandishing his axe, so that they all ducked.

Even Fungus had gone pale. "Never use that word again," he hissed, shakily. "This is the ancient hall of the dwarfs, home to strange and exotic artefacts... and substances... We do not EVER mention the V word. Got it?"

"Yes, Fungus," said Chris, unabashed. "So, what happened to this Amulet then?"

"Ah," said Lakin, who had overheard, partly as a result of the excellent acoustics in the tunnel, and partly because he was nosy, "the great sorrow of our times. The Lord Lucan vanished, wearing it, and neither has been found since. Without the Amulet, we lost our power to bar the gate that opens between worlds close to our Eastern Doors, and to completely bar the doors of Helvyndelve itself."

"Which has plenty of bars inside, anyway," put in Fungus, probably unhelpfully.

"We can no longer keep wicked things out," Lakin said remorsefully.

"Specially when it's in Fungus' pockets," muttered Haemar, with a grin.

Lakin turned, and in a rather disgusted fashion went stomping off down the corridor. A small explosion of dust surrounded each footfall until he resembled a small, animated, thundercloud.

"Hey, Haemar, I think you upset him," said Fungus.

"Might teach him something. When have we dwarfs ever tried

singing four-part acapella harmony? With these echoes? Mebbe drunk, but never sober."

"Why," whispered Linda, "would the dwarfs want a Barber Shop Quartet when they all have beards?"

"Because," answered Fungus in a low voice, "they are rubbish with guitars. See a dwarf on stage with a guitar, and you know why they call them axes."

"If either of you children are interested" came a (dusty) voice from ahead, "this is The Western Passage, part of the Great Cross Corridor that runs the full width of the Helvyndelve from West to East. From here, may passages run off and intertwine: Do you not, Children, wander off or lose our party: you may not be found again. For look, we are no longer a numerous people, and in many caverns the dust lies heavy on the dark years buried."

Linda shivered.

"Principally of course," added Dain, "because no one can be bothered to clean up."

"And we could always track your footprints in the dust, anyway," added Haemar.

Lakin, leading the party, halted, allowing them all to catch up with his thunderous dust cloud, and indulge in a barrage of coughing. The echoes ran round the chamber ahead, glimpsed dimly in the light of a few ill lit torches on the walls. "Who's there!" he demanded.

"That's meant to be my line," complained a voice from the shadows.

"Marvin's moaning again," said Haemar.

"Guard the passage they say. Challenge all who pass they say, and some sod goes and does it for you. I mean, what was the point of sending me here to stand in the dust, suffering with piles and terminal boredom, if I don't even get to do the challenge?"

Lakin started walking again. "Marvin's complaining again," he observed.

"Well, he's a Complaining Dwarf," Fungus explained to Linda.

"But they all seem to complain, all of the time," she replied.

"Wouldn't you if you were a Dwarf? And had to live here? Anyway, about five hundred years ago, after a really wild party, the Archlord of the time came up with an idea to stop it. He set up a special band of Dwarfs, whose job it was to complain about everything, so no one else had to. Didn't work of course, but they never got disbanded. Now Lakin gives them all the horrid jobs, so that they have really got something to complain about. As anyone with those jobs would complain anyway, it's quite efficient. And gets them out of the way."

As they got closer, the Guard Dwarf emerged from his recess.

"Why, Fungus, he's only got one..."

"SSSHHH. The polite term is, he's symmetrically challenged."

"What?" asked Chris, who could not see too well in the dust.

"He's only got one leg."

"That Fungus, he's got a lousy sense of humour," whispered

Haemar.

"Why?"

"Last time we had a gig the guards could come to, he made us play *At the Hop*."

Passing Marvin, the party went down a flight of stairs into a large, airy cavern. This time the space was well lit, and in front of a huge set of bronze doors stood a number of well turned out dwarfs. Unlike the symmetrically challenged Marvin, these dwarfs had all the appropriate bits, several of which were spiky, or pointy and all were very sharp. So much for the hairstyles under the helmets, they also had a number of equally sharp weapons. The Captain strode forward to meet the party. Chris and Linda could tell he was the leader, because of the huge horns on his helmet.

"Comes from putting too much moose on his hair," muttered Fungus, predictably unimpressed.

"We seek admittance to the Throne Room," said Lakin.

The Captain glowered. "You and your fellow dwarfs have the right of admittance, Lord Lakin. However, I spy strangers."

"Beginning with S?" giggled Linda.

"The Children of Men are the Wards of Grizelda of the Forth Pentangle, and I have taken them under my protection. With us travels Fungus the Troll, seeking refuge from the myrmididididions of Caer Surdin."

"Oh yeah, with bells on, I suppose. And if that's Fungus, last time he was here it took my guards four days to recover from what he gave them."

"A beating?"

"No, it was yellow and they smoked it."

"Hey, cool it man," said Fungus. "I was only being friendly, yeah? Listen, let us in an' you get an invite to the party me and Haemar are organising."

"Are you trying to bribe me?"

"I hoped I was succeeding."

"Oh, go on then. Just watch it, that's all."

The Captain made a mystical sign, involving two fingers, and the slowly the great doors, each emblazoned with a single golden rune, swung open far enough to admit one dwarf at a time.

"Still sticking, then?" Lakin asked the Captain.

"You know how it is. Ask for the maintenance team, they are always too busy."

"Running repairs, I expect."

"I'd prefer it if they stopped still long enough to do the job."

One by one therefore, they entered the Throne Room of Helvyndelve. Here at least the dust had been kept at bay, the pillars sparkled with gold leaf, and the ceiling sparkled with precious gems. Mainly because they were too high to steal without proper scaffolding, and a health and safety assessment by the light-fingered deemed them out of reach. The walls were smooth stone, with paintings of woodland scenes and famous events in the dwarfs' history. As you will not have heard of these events, there is little point in describing them, but be assured that the dwarfs all looked heroic (or constipated) and victorious.

Slowly, they walked the length of the Cavern, which lowered in height as they progressed, so that the throne at the far end seemed enormous. A large dais occupied almost the whole of the end of the Chamber.

"We held a great gig there some years ago," reminisced Fungus. "Me and the boys, we wowed them! That was when Lakin vanished you know."

"How would we know, Fungus?" asked Linda.

"Course! You weren't there. But it was a great gig."

The great Throne of the Dwarfs was built of oak wood, canopied in silver, rich with velvet, the only jarring note in the visual feast: a round hole in the backrest of the Throne.

"That hole," murmured Lakin, "is where the Amulet should be placed, that he who sits in the seat of Power can, well, wield the power of the Amulet."

At the base of the Throne stood a wooden chair, high backed, with a low backed dwarf sitting in it.

"He's the Steward," said Haemar to the teenagers.

"You mean he orders the drinks? I'm parched," Linda replied.

"Not really, but I've often seen him drunk."

The Steward stood up. "So, Lord Lakin, you have returned from your journey?"

"No, just passing through."

"Like a good curry," muttered Fungus.

"I have much to tell, though, but first, my guests are tired."

Chris opened his mouth to say that he wasn't tired, but Linda kicked his ankle, so he didn't.

"Times have changed, that we see Children of Men within the Helvyndelve."

"Indeed they have."

The Steward smiled, clearly he needed the practice. "Let them be shown to a chamber to rest. When the shadows dance on the Mere above, we shall meet again for talk."

"So he does order the drinks," said Linda, in relief. "Hope there's some food, too."

"See you're back to normal." Muttered Chris, earning another kick.

Two dwarfs led the children, and the reluctant Fungus off to a small side room. Fungus cheered up at once when he saw what was on the table.

"Your arm would have been of use here, Lord Lakin," said the Steward, severely. "The Dark Ones press us hard, and without the Amulet to hold the Doors we are unable to keep them without."

"Without what?"

"Just without."

"You can't have just without, doesn't make sense."

"Look, we have had to abandon the South Deep, for we have too little strength to hold it secure. We can be without that, if you like. The South Passage may be walked only by those with a stout heart."

"You mean you've got to be fat to go that way? How does that work then?"

"No, I mean only by the brave."

"Lets you out, then."

"Less of the abuse, Lakin. If you had been here to help, instead of taking a gap century to travel and party, we might be more secure. As it is, we have pulled away from the northern reaches of the Western Delve, though we maintain some posts there."

"Yes, we met some of the Complaining Dwarfs there."

"Got fed up of listening to them here," said Haemar.

"Whilst the Mages of Surdin argue amongst themselves, we can prevail. Yet, should one become supreme, I fear for the survival of these ancient halls," said the elderly Steward in a foreboding tone.

"One may have done so, or at least has gained some authority over some of his freres. The children are here fleeing an attack at the Vale of Tarnil, where dwells the witch Grizelda." Lakin dropped his voice to match the other's tone.

"How know you of this, when no word has reached our doors?"

"I bear the message from the post."

"Takes longer for a delivery all the time now," said Dain.

"What of these children?"

"They bear the Wards of Lingard, but seem to know not how to use them, if indeed they still have a use."

"Look cool, though," said Dain.

"Ice would look cool to you."

"Frosty, certainly, Haemar. Specially in a glass."

"You are making me feel thirsty."

"Everything makes you thirsty."

"Enough!" said the Steward. "Let us prepare for the evening meal, and we will talk further then."

"This looks brill!" said Linda, swirling a deep red cloak around her shoulders.

"May I come in?" called Lakin round the door, and entered the room.

"Hi," said Chris. "Lakin, who was that grumpy dwarf beside the Throne, then?"

"He is the Steward of Helvyndelve. Until my father is found, or declared lost forever, he rules here, and the safety of the Delve is his task. Grumpy he is, certainly, but his word runs here.

When we meet at feast, wear openly the Wards of Lingard you carry around your necks, for those he will respect."

"What do they do?"

"Who knows now, after all these years? But once they held power, and the use of that power runs in your family."

"So does madness," replied Linda, thinking of her aunt.

"Only because we are not rich enough to be eccentric," objected Chris.

"We must think about what we are to do with you. Should you chose, you might stay here for a while, else you might return to your family."

"Stay for the party, anyway," suggested Fungus.

"What party?"

"Oh, er, didn't Haemar give you an invite Lakin? I'll, er, I'll sort that out then."

"What gives?" asked Linda.

"Well, we'll play some blues an a bit of jazz, drink some stuff, smoke a bit."

"Can't do that inside now," objected Lakin. "Health and safety. You have to go outside in the rain to light up."

"But I'm naturally lit up." said the luminous troll.

"Then we will have to find some rain inside for you."

"At least I'll be singing in it."

A heavily armoured dwarf burst into the room, panting with the effort of holding all the weaponry with which he was festooned. "Lord Lakin!" gasped the dwarf.

"Yes?"

"Tidings!"

"We're nowhere near the sea."

"No, ill news."

"My Aunt's poorly again?"

"NO lord! Bodgandor have broken into the Helvyndelve at the Northern Delve, overwhelmed the guards at the rockfall and flung them back with grievous loss. They have taken the Raise Deep and First Level. The Steward and the Guards have gone to hold them before they reach the Throne Room."

"That's a downer," Fungus muttered to Haemar. "We might have to put the gig back."

"Gather our folk at the armouries," said Lakin, grimly. "For now comes the time to fight for our home."

He turned to the children. "You may well have been safer with your Aunt."

"At least she had the fridge in her kitchen," muttered Chris.

"At least she was not inside the fridge," replied Fungus. "Grizelda flavoured yoghurt." He shuddered.

"Taken Raise Deep," said Haemar. "That's bad. That's very bad."

"Why?" asked Fungus.

"Cos that's where we stashed the gear for the party…"

Lakin glared. "Then our enemies will be fuelled by more than hatred."

"Leave it out. I know some of the Lager was a bit dodgy, but calling it petrol's going a bit far."

"If you bought that Australian stuff again, calling it petrol's a compliment. I poured some on the BBQ and everything went up in flames."

"Fungus, anything you cook normally does anyway."

"It's a gift."

"Well you should give it back."

Lakin glared at them all, turned and with his heavy boots kicked a spot on the wall as hard as he could. As the cursing (and hopping on the spot) died away, a section of the wall swung outwards, and he vanished inside. A minute or so passed, at the standard rate. More cursing followed; reaching such intensity that Haemar was moved to put his hands over Linda's ears.

"I have been to Liverpool, you know," she reproved him, taking his hands off her head. He put his head in his hands.

"Kids today," sympathised Fungus. "Not as respectful as we were."

"You mean they are younger than we were before they get drunk?"

"Haemar, you were *born* drunk."

"The insults I have to bear."

"Bear with me a moment," called Lakin from the room beyond.

He then emerged, bearing a stack of short swords and helmets, which he dropped on the floor. As the echoes died away, his new clothes could be seen. Gleaming black armour, with lightning flashes.

"Oh look," said Haemar. "He's back in his black."

"Ready for some dirty deeds, then."

Lakin turned, and kicked another section of the cave wall. This time a doorway into a dark tunnel appeared. "Grab a sword each," he said. "Welcome to the highway."

"To hell?"

"To escape. This is a little used passage which will lead you to the entrance to the Western Delve, or to the Cavern of a Thousand Knights."

"Big place?" asked Chris.

"Guess how long it took to build?" asked Haemar.

"Ah, nearly three years? Because of the name?"

"No, about five years. Builders kept stopping for tea breaks. Took a thousand guards to keep them at it and finish the job."

Entering the tunnel, Lakin pointed to the left. "That way lies your route from our halls. We must go now to join the fight."

"Lakin," Linda said, "we don't want to fight, but we are not leaving, either. Maybe these silver things will help."

"Thought you were homesick," Chris muttered to her.

"Well, we can't get home, can we? And think of the story we'll have to tell at school next term," Linda replied.

"Courageous," Lakin replied.

"Bloody silly," grumbled Fungus, but the children noticed that even he had picked up a short sword. He had also grabbed a helmet, but tied that over the end of his saxophone. Lurking behind his shoulder, the helmet made him appear two headed, like a cut price Hydra. Lakin turned on his heel and led the small party along the passage. There were no lights, so Linda and Chris were grateful for the faint glow that came off Fungus – as least they could see where they could put their feet as they walked.

"Put your foot in yer mouth there," grumbled Fungus. "We could have been on the way out now. "

"Coward," Linda answered tartly.

"How quickly they grow up, these girlchildren," Heimar observed.

"Yeah, they get nasty young now," Fungus muttered back.

"I blame the parents."

"Why not? Everyone else does."

"You leave me mum out of this," Linda scolded them. Chris played to his strengths, and just looked sulky.

"Come on!" called Lakin in a commanding voice, as he led them round a bend, under a low archway and into the Cavern of a

Thousand Knights. The Cavern was not as large as the Chamber of the Throne, and clearly used as a sort of underground café, judging by the number of tables, chairs, and empty cups and glasses strewn across the floor. Despite its name, only a few hindered heavily armoured dwarfs were milling around waiting. One stepped forward, wandered across a large expanse of the floor until he was within speaking distance. Then he bowed.

"Lord," he addressed Lakin, who bowed back. "They fight now under Sirral Edge and Lower Man. We slay ten for each one of us who falls, yet they are too many and so we fall back. Most grievous, the Steward himself has been slain. His body lies in the Chamber before the Throne of Kings."

"Who leads the fighting now?"

"Lord Hemal."

"Good. Are my Guard here?"

"We are, Lord," called an assorted group of the most heavily beweaponed dwarfs Linda had seen so far. She wondered aloud how they could move.

"Slowly," whispered Fungus in her ear.

"Right!" said Lakin, looking as fierce as his guards. "Remember all of you! A fight doesn't tell you who's right, just who's left. And that's going to be us. Got it?"

"Who is goin' to tell them that?" asked Haemar, as with a lot of yelling a host of their enemy pushed their way into the far end of the Cavern.

With a lot of shouting and shoving, the dwarfs formed

themselves into a line, with Fungus noticeably to the rear. Chris and Linda found themselves pushed alongside him. Lakin drew a huge breath. After a pause, in which his face turned bright red (a nice contrast to the luminous green of Fungus, and so reminiscent of a faulty traffic light,) he yelled at the top of his voice: "BE STILL!!!"

The noise died away, as it often will for anyone capable of yelling exclamation marks – a sure sign of either a deranged mind or a policeman after Crowd Control Training Courses. A toss up which is the more dangerous to the general public.

"I am the Lord Lakin, Archlord of the Helvyndelve." Lakin continued, but with the volume control backed off somewhat: "If you leave now, you may go with your lives."

"Rather go with your life, shortarse!" came a snappy reply from a huge Bodgandor, with red and black armour, a long sword and a bad attitude.

Lakin snarled, and leapt – the Bodgandor swung the long sword in a vicious arc, but Lakin caught the blow on his shield and stabbed forward. His enemy fell, the sword in its chest. Linda covered her eyes. In front, the horde of Bodgandor snarled, and a storm of spears rained around the dwarfs, clattering off their shields and helmets. Then the cavern shook to the sound, almost below hearing, of heavy feet stamping towards the fight from the darkened passages beyond.

A blast of red light lit the cavern.

"Hey, Haemar, we could use that at the next gig," said Fungus.

"It's better than that cheap light show you bought from Grizelda, that's for sure."

Three enormous Trolls entered the fray, the ground trembling beneath their feet, and not just from their foot odour. The dwarfs muttered amongst themselves, and stepped back apace.

"Three trolls! We are lost!" cried a dwarf at the back of the group.

"Speak for yourself," answered Fungus. "I know exactly where I am. Course, I might not like it much, but I know where I am."

"In trouble normally," observed Haemar.

"Or causing it more like," muttered the dwarf next to him.

"Why are you worried?" asked Chris, who was brandishing his sword and looking as belligerent as a Manchester United fan at Liverpool's football ground.

"Problem is," Haemar told him, "there are three trolls there and they are just too damn hard to kill off. Basically being walking rocks, it needs a decent length of time with a hammer and chisel to do them any damage, and whilst you are on the job, they might just object."

"Lakin isn't panicking."

"Well, you know what they say about someone who doesn't panic at a crisis."

"What?"

"They probably don't understand what's going on," muttered Fungus, rummaging madly in his rucksack.

"What are you doing?" Linda hissed at him. She did not like the look of the menacing trolls, and felt fully prepared to panic.

"Trolls have one weakness. They are hard to hurt, but can be poisoned, as they are seriously greedy. And I have something here that might help." Fungus, showing the enthusiasm he normally reserved for a Barry Manilow album, pushed towards the front line of dwarfs. Carefully putting his sax down, he lobbed some misshapen objects towards the trolls, who with wild cries grabbed them out of the air – and ate the offerings. There was a long silence, and then one troll fell backwards and stopped moving. A second fell to its knees, and bowing forward head banged the floor, which shook. The third just froze on the spot.

"What did you give them?" asked Chris.

"Something yer aunt made – rock cakes with added herbs."

"What herbs?"

"Even when you get to fifty you will be too young to know…"

"We've all got to live that long first," muttered the dwarf next to them, as with a yell the Bodgandor jumped forward again.

"Steady!" Chris warned a medium sized specimen who landed in front of him with a raised sword. "If you hit me with that, I'll call Childline."

But the dwarfs had been released from their fear by Fungus's inventive attack, and the battle surged past the stricken trolls until with despairing wails the Bodgandor turned and fled back through the doors and down the broad stairs leading out of the Cavern. Lakin strode forward, and the dwarfs followed him. Some paused to add dropped swords or spears to their already impressive collection: but as they reached the doors, red flames grew at the bottom of the stairs and smoke rose all around the group, coiling into unpleasant shapes.

"They have lit the Fires of Surdin beneath us!" exclaimed Haemar.

"I have a foreforeboding," grumbled a small dwarf who stood next to Chris.

"Why four? Can't you have a two boding, or a five boding?"

"Well you could," Fungus told him, "but four-four has the best rhythm."

"Maybe for the blues. But you're green."

"None of us can help how we are made."

"Why not? Even dwarfs can have surgery."

"Plastic surgery?" asked Linda, who felt in need of a distraction.

"Well, engraving or maybe metal refinishing."

Lakin had decided to take stock of the situation. "You!" he barked at an inoffensive dwarf standing nearby. "Go and find out what is happening in the upper levels, and elsewhere in the Helvyndelve." The dwarf bowed and scurried off. Lakin turned to Fungus. "Good move with those Trolls, I thought we might have been in trouble then."

"It was nothing," said Fungus, with false modesty.

"Was it? OK then I won't mention it again." Lakin hurried off towards the small returning dwarf, eager for news. Fungus looked a bit disgruntled.

"Right," Lakin said urgently to his small messenger. "What's the news, short version?"

"No need to be rude. Just cos I'm little."

"Be brief."

"OK, OK. We've still got the upper levels, and the Guard Captain there has managed to shut the Doors, so no Bodgandor can get there. Course, we can't either at the moment. Lord Hemal still holds the Second Deep, so we have some power and lights, but there is a horde around him, and he is be-sieged."

"Seiged by bees?"

"No, Bodgandor."

"OK then." Lakin raised his voice, so that he could be more widely heard. "Some here will hold the North Passage, so that we may pass between the various halls of the Delve. The rest will come with me, and we will gain the Central Delve, and the Hall of the Throne." Calmly, Lakin allotted various dwarfs to the tasks he had chosen for them.

"How can he be so calm?" wondered Chris. Fungus gave him a sour look.

"We've done that one."

Behind them, clearly visible through the open doors of the cavern, came another blast of red light.

"Blast!" cried Lakin. "But that is their job! Come on!" The dwarfs began running, something Chris had thought impossible with all the weight they were carrying. Down the long corridor they went at some pace, with the echoes of their running feet running all around them, a sound that was to haunt Linda's nightmares. After some time, the group arrived at another meeting of passages, held by half a dozen very nervous guards. They had been very nervous, not supposed to leave their post, and the evidence was clear. Or, to be more accurate, rather cloudy.

"At the heart of the Helvyndelve, under the mighty peak itself lies the Central Delve." Lakin explained to Linda, as she panted for breath, and regretted it. "Four caverns lie there; Topmost is the Grand Cavern, to which all the Main Passages run, below that the Chamber of the Throne, then the Cavern of a Thousand Knights, and lowest the Great Deep, which can only be reached from the Second Deep of the Northern Delve, so although that part is presently lost to us, if we can seal off the Northern Delve we can hold the rest of the Helvyndelve safe, and then recover the Deeps.."

"It's all too deep for me." Chris was less out of breath than his sister, but more out of his depth.

"This way," Lakin pointed to one passageway with his spear, nearly impaling one of the nervous Guards as he did so, "will lead to the Chamber of the Throne. That way" - he swung the spear back to the other direction, causing another guard to duck urgently- "will rise back up to the Grand Cavern." He glared at the doubled over dwarf beside him. "Why do you keep bowing like that?"

"Your spear keeps hitting me on the helmet, Lord."

"Right. Linda, listen to me. You carry a silver necklace, called a Ward. I do not know its use, though it is rumoured to have had power aeons ago."

"What's Ian got to do with it?" *

[* Just goes to show really, that there is no joke so bad that others cannot copy it.]

"I said *aeons,* not *Ians,* Fungus. Try to be more helpful. Linda, I was told to tell you, if in need, hold the silver thing, look at the charm, and if any word can be seen there, speak it. More than that I know not."

"What sort of word?" asked Chris.

"'Ian' probably," suggested Fungus, who was out of breath and still feeling unhelpful, earning a glare from Lakin.

From behind them, in the darkened passage, came the sound of fighting. Several of the guards drew their swords, and moved quietly to stand between Lakin and the threat, but as they did so, a group of swarthy ill-omened Bodgandor came towards them, driving before them the remnants of the guards they had overwhelmed. Spears hissed through the air, then Lakin's personal guards joined the fray, and the danger passed. Lakin left them to it, and began to run with the rest of the dwarfs crowding around Chris and Linda for their protection. Poor Fungus was left out to follow on as best he could. On and on they went, and at last emerged in a hallway full of dwarfs. A challenge, a response, and the party passed into the Chamber of the Throne.

The hall was no longer empty, as it had been before, but now full of jostling, complaining dwarfs, all preparing to fight. As the last of Lakin's guards came through the Doors, they were closed, and barred with great timbers and heavy swearing. By the Throne lay a still shape, and close by stood a solitary dwarf.

Lakin walked the length of the room, and embraced dwarf as if they were brothers. Well, actually, they were brothers, so naturally they were not that keen on each other. When they were fed up with looking at each other, they turned to look at the still body beside them.

CHAPTER SIX.

"He died well," said Heimdall.

"So did he. We may get our chance too. We should seal the Northern Delve now, whilst there is time."

"That is for Hemal to decide."

"He is under siege in the Second Deep. We are not, so I say we seal the passages now."

"Too late, Lords," called a dishevelled and dusty dwarf, carrying a riven shield and a tired expression. "The upper levels are in the hands of our foes."

"But there were six hundreds of you there!" exclaimed Lakin, to the small dust heap in front of him, which doubled as a dwarf.

"And we slew them, and slew them, and slew them. But then came a sorcerer, who laughed at our arms,* and blasted us with the fires of Surdin, until those who could fell back to the Grand Cavern. There they stand, but the Passages of Helvyndelve are in the hands of Caer Surdin."

[* He meant the weapons of course. Even evil sorcerers have to be careful of offending ethnic minorities. And dwarfs are a minority, owing to their size.]

"A Sorcerer!" exclaimed Linda. "Could this be Ned coming for us again?"

"Possible," agreed Lakin. Fungus looked even more gloomy, and started rummaging in his backpack for something to lighten the mood.

"You look tense," Chris said to him.

"I'm not tense. Just very, very alert. Can't you tell this is a time when we need all the lerts we can get?"

"Take heart!" demanded Lakin. "All is not lost!"

"If it's not lost, where is it then?"

"What?"

"This all that isn't lost. Where is it then?"

"Shut up Fungus."

Moodily, Fungus pulled a bottle out of his backpack and took a long drink.

Linda gave him a severe look of disapproval.

"Hey, remember the greatest scientific saying ever," he said to her.

"E=MC Squared?"

"All problems are soluble in beer."

Then came three heavy blows on the sealed Doors behind them. The chamber went quiet, and Lakin strode towards the Doors.

"Open Sesame!" came a voice from the other side of the Doors.

"Get Lost!" yelled back Lakin.

"Snappy repartee eh?" contributed Fungus.

"Open Sesame," repeated the menacing voice.

"Doesn't he know, that only works with Thieves?" remarked Heimar.

"And there's more than forty of us here."

"But who's counting?"

"And of course all dwarfs are honest."

"Natch."

Outside in the passage, the three trolls started a literary discussion.

"Should ave opened when I said that." #1

"Nah, fink you got the wrong un. Try ABRACADABRA." #2

"Nothing appened." # 3

"Well, you didn't try it, did you?" # 2

"You said it though." # 1

"I thought *you* ad to say it." # 2

"Nah." # 1

"ABRACADABRA then." # 2

"Still didn't work." #3

"Worth a try though. Anyone got any more opening spells?"#2

"I got one." # 3

"Give it a go, then." # 1

"MEL-LON" # 3 (the literary one, who had read Lord of the Rings. Or at least, watched the first part of the film, once.)

"Isn't that a fruit?" # 2

"What, like a blackberry?" # 1

"I've got a Blackberry." # 2

"Try that then." # 3

"Can't. Don't get a signal down here." # 2

"Typical. All that money and the technology still won't work when you want it." # 3

"Back to traditional ways then. Just give it a kick." # 1

"Won't work if you do that. It's only made of plastic." # 2

"The door, you idiot." # 1

"Oh, right." # 2

The troll raised his right foot, and gave the doors a serious kick. So much dust fell all around that the three trolls vanished from view. "Don't they ever clean anything round ere?"# 3

The dust cloud vanished as if by magic (which it was) as a robed figure came round a bend in the corridor and approached the trolls. The sorcerer, for it was he, opened his mouth to unleash a barrage of abuse, but indulged in some Olympic standard coughing instead.

"All those cigarettes." # 2

"Bet he never read the health warnings." # 3

"Give that door some welly." # 1 urgently, having seen the expression under the hood.

"Not got me wellies on. Put me big boots on instead today." # 3.

"Don't be too big for them. Just kick that door down." # 1

Again, the Doors shook to the impact. All three Trolls stood together, linked arms and (with an uncanny resemblance to the dancers from the Folies Bergere review shows,) gave the Doors a simultaneous boot. With a crack and a groan, the bars holding the Doors shut gave way, and as the Trolls fell backwards with the reaction, Bodgandor swarmed under the archway, then stopped, when faced by the still, silent rows of dwarfs. Having lumbered less than gracefully to their feet, the Trolls entered more cautiously.

"Not bad in ere, is it? Think we'll ave this as a place to kip down." # 1

"Your sleep will be a long one, Troll," snarled Lakin.

"Was that a threat, do you think?" # 2

"Not a very good one, was it. Do you want to try again Shorty?"# 3

"Do not bandy words with me, Troll, for I am not happy."

"No? Which one are you then?"# 3

With a yell, Lakin sprang at the troll with his sword raised. An iron mace met the sword; the sound of the clash filled the whole cavern. Released by the noise, the dwarfs sprang at the

Bodgandor, and the chamber filled with slashing, yelling screaming figures. The children crouched down on the dais, behind a large shield held in place by Fungus, who had pulled the largest he could find out of a wall display of antiques. It was probably a valuable heirloom, but (having no heir) he preferred to loom behind it.

"Why don't you go to help them?" Chris hissed at Fungus.

"I promised yer Aunt to look after yer, an even now I'm more scared of her than of that lot."

Lakin's fight with the Troll was not going well. The other two Trolls kept making rude remarks, and now the superior strength of the Troll was driving Lakin back towards the Dais where the children and Fungus waited.

"Ho!" shouted the Troll, in triumph, as Lakin stumbled and fell backwards on the steps leading to the Throne. Linda, felt a blaze of ice shoot through her body, and stared at the charm around her neck: a strange word shone like emerald against the silver. A new feeling of strength flooded her mind.

"Gotcha!" cried the Troll, and raised his Iron Mace high to strike.

In her head, then aloud, Linda cried the word revealed: a shaft of green light sped from the ward of Lingard and struck the Troll, outlining its whole body in green light. Fungus shuddered in sympathy. The Troll was lifted from his feet, and thrown across the entire chamber to strike the wall beside the Doors. The other two Trolls stepped quickly back out of the Chamber of the Throne, and seeing them retreat, the Bodgandor turned too, and fled.

"Linda, thank you," panted Lakin as he drew breath. He looked in approval as the dwarfs swung the great Doors back closed, and began piling blocks of fallen stones behind them and over the fallen Troll. "How did you do that?"

"I don't know," said Linda in shock.

"That was awesome!" exclaimed Chris. "Do you think mine will do that, too?"

"I don't know," said Lakin.

"Brother," said Heimdall, approaching the dais. "You have made a good beginning."

"Well, it's a start. Brother, will you take some of our folk here to stiffen the resolve of those on the higher levels, and hold at worst the Western passage so that if all else fails we will have a way out?"

"Yes, Brother, I shall. Until we meet again." Heimdall and Lakin embraced, briefly, then the former left, calling to his guards to follow him. One raised his voice in song, only to be drowned in a chorus of complaints. "No more bloody HIHO!"

"But, chief, it's expected."

"Not by me. If you must sing, can't you find something better?"

"What do you suggest?"

"Falling off a rock."

"Seasick Steve?"

"I've never been Seasick."

Fungus sat on the side of the dais, and started playing a slow blues on his saxophone.

Haemar joined him. "*Summertime. The living is easy*", he sang, slowly.

Lakin gave them a long look, but then turned to Linda.

"Are you sure you do not know what you did to use the Ward?"

"Actually, Lakin, it felt more as though the Ward used me."

"That could well be the case. These things are Old Magic, and there are no instructions for them."

"Bit like the last self assembly kitchen units our dad got. There were no instructions with those, either. And the doors fell off after a week."

"These are the Wards of Lingard," said Lakin, trying to be solemn. "They should not be taken lightly."

"Mine feels quite light," Chris told him.

"Has anyone told you anything about them?" Linda asked.

"Erald told me a little, but I hesitate to teach you. Chris, have you ever fought before today?"

"Only at school, or at the football match."

"Then you did well. Oh, I wish Erald was here, for I do not know enough of that dark wizard to be able to fight him."

"We know him. It's Ned, isn't it?"

"Yes, Linda it is."

"Well, he's twice tried to capture us now."

"What else do you know?"

"He drinks Guinness, and swears a lot."

"Interesting, but not a lot of help. Fungus, what do you know of him?"

The green troll put down the sax and thought. "Besides his Guinness intake?"

"Does he have any bad habits?"

"His clothing?"

On the other side of the (now closed) doors, heated discussions could be heard, by anyone who could hear through several feet of solid rock. Or, of course, were present to listen first hand.

"Simmer down," Troll # 2 told Ned.

"Don't get so fired up." Troll # 3.

"He's like a cat on a hot tin roof." Troll #2

"Boiling mad."

"Steaming."

"Fuming."

"Hopping."

"All right, enough of the second rate comedy."

"Second rate? We won an award last year."

"I don't want to know what for. Shut up, or you'll get what for."

"He could join in, you know. With comments like that."

"It's a thought."

"No it's not. Thought is something that don't seem to enter yer heads. Why did yer leave the other Troll in there? An' how come yer ran away, anyway?"

The two Trolls looked at each other for inspiration. "Did you not see what happened to our Brother? Whatever they had was able ter throw him across a room. Would you have fancied being on the receiving end of that?"

"What about yer mate? Do you leave yer people in there?"

"Listen, you muppet, either he's dead (sob!) In which case it don't matter, or else he's going to wake up in a little while, with a terrible hangover."

"And we know what he's like when he has a hangover, and don't want to be near him."

"Nor will those dwarfs, so we'll get back in there when he opens the doors for us. Just make sure that you've got something to drink ready when that happens."

"Why? Will it calm him down?"

"No, but it won't hurt you so much when he hits you."

"He's got a short fuse."

"Isn't that dwarfs?"

"They've got short everything."

Ned ignored both the Trolls, and pulled out the enchanted silver compass he had been given. He then became quite agitated, as the dial reacted sharply.

"He's started hopping again," said Troll #2

"Right," said Ned.

"Time for a cuppa is it?"

"Our target is that way."   Ned pointed at the Doors.

"What, again?" #3

"Bin there, dun that." #2

"No you didn't, cos yer came out with nowt." Ned turned to the Bodgandor, who were sat around further down the passage, swapping lurid stories of the fighting so far and comparing scars, swords and complaints. "Right, you lot. The Trolls are going to get the Doors open again, an' then we're all goin through."

"Do we have to?"

"You want me to make yer?"

"You and whose army?"

"These two Trolls for a start. Yer all know that the Grey Mage gave me our orders. Wanna take it up with him?"

There was a lot of despondent grumbling, but the Bodgandor picked up various weapons and formed up without much order, enthusiasm, or personal hygiene. Ned nodded grimly, stowed the silver compass away in a handy pocket and glared at the Trolls. Troll # 3 wandered up to the Doors, and knocked politely, twice.

"What in the Seven Hells do you think you are doing?" screamed Ned.

"Exploring all the avenues. They might want to give in without a fight."

"Sounds good to us," agreed the evil horde of Bodgandor.

"Besides," grinned Troll #2 nastily, "we wanna see if #1 wakes up inside there."

Inside the Chamber of the Throne, the atmosphere was a little frosty. Fungus had suggested that, if the fighting had stopped, perhaps they should have the gig anyway. Haemar had agreed, as had Felldyke. As Felldyke was the drummer however, his opinion carried little weight. Unlike Felldyke, who was almost spherical.

"Look," Lakin explained, "there's a war on!"

"Good for the morale then," Fungus replied.

"Haemar's singing is good for morale? It's frightening!"

"Well, maybe it will frighten Them too. Then They'll go away."

"We've got dwarfs fighting here!"

"Only to get in without tickets," Fungus retorted.

"Errrr," muttered Felldyke, which in the universal language of music, all understood.

(Tickets? What tickets? Oh *those* tickets. The ones you asked me to sell? Well, sort of, I never quite got round to it, you see. How many? Well, in round terms, sort of, all of them. Any of them. None of them. If you see what I mean. Will next Monday do? No? Oh. Sorry….) Errrr is like a short hand version.

"FREE?" Haemar reeled. Fungus sat down, looking pale.

"What's wrong with that?" asked Chris.

"I'm a professional musician." Fungus panted. "NO ONE asked the King to play for free."

"Nixon did."

"And look what happened to him." He glared at Lakin, who was sniggering. "Take heed of that example."

"I'd like to hear you play," said Linda. Fungus beamed, recovering his good nature.

"Oh well, who've we got? Me, of course, Haemar, Felldyke, any more?"

"Scar is around somewhere, and his spare organ has been behind the dais for more years than I can count."

"Spare organ? What sort of organ?" asked Chris, who, like Elvis, had a suspicious mind.

"The sort of organ a has been can leave lying around. Cheap keyboard, really."

Lakin decided he had better organise some food and drink (the latter getting an enthusiastic reception), and so Fungus and Haemar started setting up their kit.

From the heap of dwarfs against the wall a battered specimen (who turned out to be Scar) stumbled towards the dais, looking in need of several spare organs. Haemar pulled a well used harmonica from one of his several pockets, Felldyke struck out for the drum kit, making contact on only the third attempt, and together they started a slow number, which seemed familiar, and gathered pace. Lakin groaned.

"What are they playing?" Linda asked.

"In The Hall of the Mountain King." Lakin replied. "Listz."

"Bless you."

"That's the composer, not a sneeze. Franz Listz.* I dunno, that Fungus has no sense of occasion. Look," the beat moved up tempo somewhat, "now they're on the Velvet Underground."

[* Actually, Greig wrote In the Hall of the Mountain King. But it's hard to be an expert in Classical Music when you live under a Fell in the Lake District and can only get reception from Radio 1.]

"I'm waiting for the dwarf," sang Haemar, with feeling.

"I'm waiting for the end," muttered Lakin.

"Actually, they're not bad," said Linda. Most of the dwarfs seemed to agree, and started to cluster round in front of the impromptu stage.

"Why is Haemar swaying from side to side as he sings?" asked

Linda.

"A moving target is harder to hit," answered Lakin.

The band was now starting to get in the swing, and was playing a boogie with some verve. Several dwarfs were now up and dancing, and Chris and Linda joined them.

"We're not the first to play in a Cavern, but I reckon we are better than those insects," panted Fungus.

"That's it for a bit," warbled Haemar, finally pausing for breath and applause. Felldyke then took a deep breath, and started to attack his drum kit as if its presence offended him, at least as much as it offended the others in the band.

"Drum break," Haemar said, sitting down beside Chris.

"Certainly sounds like he's trying to break them."

"He once heard Keith Moon do a five minute solo, and has been jealous of it ever since." The sound of the drum kit's active resistance echoed and re echoed round the cavern. Fungus sat down beside them, whilst Scar slumped to the floor beside his organ. No one in the Cavern noticed a pile of rocks beside the unguarded Doors rock in time to the beat, and then fall over as a Troll emerged from the heap and looked around blearily. One huge hand shot out for balance, and fell on the handles. The Doors began to open, the sound lost in the cacophony. Fungus got up slowly.

"I think either he's finishing off, or giving up. How about *'Light my Fire'*? The band got onto the dais, and after kicking Scar to life, set into their version of the number. The crowd were appreciative, and showed it in the traditional dwarf manner.

"See?" pointed out Lakin. "Harder to hit."

"Who did this one?" asked Linda

"The Doors," replied Chris

"The Doors!" yelled Lakin, looking round.

"That's what I said."

"And I heard you. Even over Them."

"Wasn't Them. It was the Doors played this one."

"No, the Doors! Look!"

Troll #! Had opened the Doors as Troll #3 raised his hand for a second time. Instead of knocking, less politely, he had managed to thump his fellow Troll on the nose. Troll #1 fell backwards pulling the Doors wide open. The Bodgandor flooded in, surprising and scattering the dwarfs who were not in a condition to put up a co ordinated defence. Most of the dwarfs were still clustered around the band: who took one look at the crowd invasion and decided to beat it. Fungus paused only to grab (in strict order) his sax, then Linda and Chris before deciding to do a runner. And without getting paid!

"Once in a lifetime gig," Fungus panted, heading for the rear exit.

"Never again," agreed Haemar, picking up a third hand sword as he ran, and brushing the third hand off the hilt and onto the floor.

At the far end of the Chamber, they turned. Felldyke and Scar were with the party, and close by were Lakin and his guards, who had also decided that discretion carried better survival prospects. Further back in the cavern a number of dwarfs were feeling annoyed that the gig had been interrupted, and were expressing those feelings in order to avoid possible psychological issues later in life as a result of repressed hostility. The noise was deafening, even after Felldyke's drumming.

Felldyke shook his head, causing dandruff to fly from his beard over a wide area. "No rhythm."

"And you would know?"

From the passage behind them came a battered and slightly scorched dwarf, looking like the product of inferior concert catering.

"Is Lord Lakin here?"

Lakin stepped towards the dwarf, without taking his eyes off the fight.

"Lord Heimdall sends to tell you that he is sorely pressed above, with assaults from both the North and South. He says he needs help to hold the West Passage."

Lakin looked with a critical eye at the brawl in the cavern. It was hard to tell if anyone was winning, or losing. Apart from losing the odd body part, or a lot of tempers, of course. However, at the far end the Trolls appeared to be having some small success in awakening their felled colleague.

"You thumped me!" said #1

"Ah, but it were an accident, honest." #2

"How can it be an accident? You thumped me on the nose!"

"Ah, well, I were tryin' to hit the Door."

"I'm a Troll, not a Door. Can't you see the difference?"

"I were only tryin' to open the Door."

"Next time, turn the handle."

"Weren't a handle. Was a knob."

"Then next time turn the knob on your side!"

"I thought were talkin about the Door?"

Ned sidestepped the discussion, and slipped into the Cavern. He held the silver compass, which was pointing steadily in one direction now. Stealthily, he moved forward, whilst walking sideways to keep his back to the wall. As a comic turn it had some advantages; as a means of progress, it just made him look like a bigger prat. However, with all the yelling and clamour of the fight he stayed unnoticed until he had crept around the dais to the back.

"Hey! You!" yelled Lakin at him.

"Is that Ned?" Chris asked Fungus.

"Nah. Looks nothing like him."

Ned threw back the cowl as he peered more closely at the silver compass.

"On the other hand, it could be I suppose."

Lakin drew his sword, and walked towards Ned, who kicked the travel box for Scar's organ apart.

"Oi!" Scar yelled." That's mine, you git!"

"You left it there for years after that gig we did here," Haemar pointed out, "and never came to look at it."

"Yeah, well, it was me spare, wasn't it?"

Ned bent down, and with a yell of triumph, jumped up with something dangling from his hand.

"That's the Amulet!" shouted Lakin, and chased Ned back down the length of the Cavern.

"What Amulet?" said Scar, puzzled.

"The Amulet of Kings!" said Haemar, in awe. "It was in your case all along."

"I didn't think it was that long since I used my organ."

"Is that the Amulet Lakin was telling us about?" asked Chris, confused.

"Yeah, and Lakin won't be happy that Ned found it first."

Lakin was indeed not happy (we established that last chapter) but grumpy, and was proving it with language unfit to print even under specialist cover and brown paper wrapping. But Ned, with glee, and with some ceremony, put the chain of the Amulet over his head and then slid past the squabbling Trolls into the passage behind them. He called out, and the Bodgandor disengaged from the dwarfs they were fighting, and retreated to the Doors to the Cavern, leaving the dwarfs to fight amongst themselves. A few of them hardly noticed the difference. Lakin sank down, and put his head in his hands. "It is lost." He wailed.

"Can't we get it back?" asked Linda.

"How will we find it?" asked Chris, trying to be helpful.

Fungus tried to help, too. "You know the best way to find something? Buy a replacement."

"It's The Amulet of Kings! You can't just nip down to the supermarket and pick up another one!" yelled Lakin.

"Oh. Sorry. What about that jeweller's in Keswick?"

"No."

"Take them a picture, bet they could make one."

"It would not have the magical powers of the original."

"What exactly are they, then?" asked Linda.

"Once the wearer has carried out a ceremony in a secret chamber in Helvyndelve, he can control all the Doors, the lights, and the power that runs the Delve. Since it was lost, for example, non of the rubbish has been collected."

"Not because you dwarfs were bone idle then?" asked Fungus.

"It doesn't help. But worse, the Amulet can be used to open some of the Gates Between Worlds. At present, a wizard of Caer Surdin has opened a Gate and brought these Bodgandor through, but the magician will not be able to keep it open for very long. The Amulet could keep such a Gate open for as long as the wearer willed, and Surdin could bring many allies to their aid." Lakin pulled himself together, and rallied his despondent dwarfs to stop hitting each other.

"Good dwarf in a crisis," Haemar observed.

"Yup."

"Still, you know what they say."

"I think I know this one already."

"Anyone good in a crisis, has found someone else to blame."

They all looked at Scar.

"Why are you all looking at me?"

"Because," said Lakin in his ear, "the Lost Amulet was lost – and found -in a music case of yours. Would you care to tell me why?"

"Errrr…"

"When did you put it there?"

"I didn't."

"Then what is your explanation?"

"Errr…"

"I don't think that's going to be good enough."

"To be fair, Lord," said Felldyke, "I know he hasn't been near that case in an age. Maybe Lord Lucan put it there before he left? For safekeeping?"

"Errr."

"Can anyone else vouch for that?"

"Me," said Fungus. "That case has been there since that big gig we did here for Lord Lucan's party. You know, the one where you and that nice witch with the long legs and fancy broomstick were found playing sardines? Without a frying pan?"

"Out of the frying pan into the fire eh?" suggested Haemar.

"That was the one where Lucan went AWOL," put in Scar eagerly, now he could see he was off the hook, or at least not yet impaled on it.

"I recall it," said Lakin, curtly.

"Bet you do," sniggered Fungus.

"Bet she does too," added Haemar.

"So, if we didn't know it was there, how did that wizard from Surdin?"

"Good question," mused Lakin.

"Got a good answer?" asked Fungus.

"Not yet. But I will have, when I get me hands on that Ned."

The Doors to the Chamber were still blocked by the three Trolls, who had not yet settled their disagreement, but were yet open. More yelling followed by an awful scream could be heard. The scream became higher pitched, and carried on for some time.

Fungus listened, impressed. "We could use those vocals next time we do *'Man on a Silver Mountain'*."

"Are you saying I'm not good enough?"

"No Haemar, but as a dwarf, you're just too short to reach that high register."

"I can try."

"What are you gonna do, sing from a chair?"

"He'd need a stepladder," suggested Felldyke.

The scream again dopplered around the Chamber, raising echoes and repeating quadrophonically.

"Stepladder's not enough," said Scar. "We'd need an effects board to do that."

"Did yer hear that?" called Ned, through the Doors.

"How on earth does he expect anyone to miss it?" asked Chris.

"That was your Lord Heimdall."

"Didn't know he could sing like that," Fungus said to Lakin.

"Would you like him back? He's no longer in mint condition, I'm afraid, but he is still quite serviceable – at the moment."

Lakin ground his teeth.

"Just give me those two menchildren, and you can have (what's left of him) back."

"Us?" Linda asked Lakin, confused and frightened. "Why us?"

"He's been after us since we got here," said Chris, grimly. "Maybe we should ring Child Protection."

"The Council don't come down here." Lakin told him.

"We know that. There's no holes in the pavements," Chris told him. "And I haven't seen one reflective jacket. The only thing that glows in the dark is Fungus."

"Mind you, the Performing Rights Society turned up to demand fees from us for playing a radio at work," commented Haemar.

"Yeah, but they get everywhere. Must have a special pass."

"So why us?" Linda asked again.

"The only thing I can think of, is that he wants these things we are wearing," said Chris.

"Of course," said Lakin. "The Wards of Lingard. He must want their power."

"Well he's not having them. This is the first decent bit of jewellery I've had."

"But Chris, it makes you look like a footballer."

"Spot on," muttered Fungus. "Thick and idle."

"I'd take rich, thick and idle any day," answered Chris.

Again, the high scream, with overtones of agony over a solid foundation of discomfort with a side flavour of distress echoed through the Doors. Several of the dwarfs flinched.

"I think that he's impatient for an answer," called Ned.

Linda began to cry.

"Prove you have him," called back Lakin.

"Nah, but you could come an' see for yourself if you want."

"Don't go," Fungus told Lakin. "They could have sampled that sound from a Black Sabbath album."

"They'd better pay them royalties if they have."

Lakin grabbed some nearby spears, clearly intending to do something brave or foolhardy (often interchangeable terms) but hesitated when a group of dwarfs came running into the Chamber from a side passage from the South Delve, yelling loudly – or at least as loudly as they could after a lot of fighting and yelling. Wheezing frantically, possibly.

"Flee, before you are trapped!"

Lakin grabbed a passing dwarf, and forced an explanation from him, as the remainder headed off through the Doors behind Fungus, heading for the Great Cavern and the Western passage. "Tell me!" he snarled.

"There were just too many for us. We were the last to get out of the South Delve, though many went to join Lord Heimdall, who commands in the Central Delve." The dwarf stopped to get some breath.

"See?" put in Fungus. "I said it was sampled."

"Don't think it was Sabbath though," said Scar. "Maybe one of them trash metal bands."

"Yer mean *Thrash* metal bands don't yer?"

"Nah. Don't like it me self."

"The whole of the North and South Delves are now lost to us," carried on the wheezing dwarf, sounding like a punctured accordion. "Only the Central Delve and Western Passage are left."

Lakin made his plan quickly. "Brothers," he yelled, causing many dwarfs to look at him in some bemusement. They were not related to him. "Yes, brothers, for we are a family!"

"Well, they certainly argue enough," muttered Fungus to Linda.

"Now we must fight for our right…"

"To party?" Fungus suggested unhelpfully, as Lakin drew breath

"To live in our own Halls in peace. Go you now to Lord Heimdall, we will hold the Central Delve, regroup, and then chase these curs out of our home!"

The dwarfs clashed their swords on their shields, and began to form up.

"My guards and I will hold here, and Lord Heimdall will lead the counter attack!"

The dwarfs cheered him, and then marched out of the Chamber of the Throne. Lakin watched them leave, and then turned. "You lot, stand still!" he snarled at the musicians, who were starting to follow the other dwarfs out of the Cavern. "Special Duties."

"Who died and made him King?" Felldyke asked Scar.

"His father, I suppose."

"Oh. Right."

"Now," ordered Lakin, still in decisive mode, "we need to block those Doors." He pointed at the far end of the cavern, where the Great Doors still stood open, but no presence of enemies remained except for one Troll still sat on the ground.

"OK Lord," said one enterprising guard. "We can shove the Doors shut, break the locks when closed, then build a barrier behind them from that rubble."

"Good thinking. Let's get on with it."

The dwarfs ran towards the Doors, and ignoring the Troll who was now leaning back against one Door, slammed the other closed and operated the locks. Lakin hammered the Locks then with his axe, until they were unlikely to work again: meanwhile, working with speed and skill unlike anything Chris or Linda had seen them display before, the rubble was piled against the Doors to form a high barrier.

"That will do nicely," said Lakin, as he led them back towards the Throne.

"I dunno," muttered the remaining Troll, from his place deep within the rubble. "I think I'm just another brick in their wall."

"OK," Lakin began, as he looked around his chosen band (and shuddered slightly.) His guards stood solidly, with battered shields and well used swords. Linda and Chris stood next to each other, nervous and a little bewildered still at how their lives had spiralled into this weird situation. Fungus and his band hung around at one side, also nervous (and as bewildered as musicians often look when deprived of instruments, an audience or something to drink.). "Our task now is to recover the Amulet of Kings." Lakin paused, hoping to get a reaction. Cheering or applause would have suited him well: but neither was forthcoming.

"How do we do that?" asked Linda.

"Well, to use the Amulet, the Wearer must attune himself…"

"What about herself? Or Itself, if unsure?" asked Fungus, receiving a glare.

"Attune himself to the Ways of Power, which can only be achieved by a ceremony in a Secret Place of Power. A true mage will need little time once there."

"Where is this place, then?" asked Felldyke.

"Why don't we know about this Place, then?" asked Haemar.

"Because it is a secret, idiot. But as heir to Lord Lucan, I know."

"Well, how will this Ned found out then?"

"Dunno. But he found the lost Amulet, which we had all been searching after for years, so bets are that he can find the Place of Power."

"As heir to Lucan, I have already been partly attuned, so if we can recover the Amulet I will have partial power over the Amulet, and be able to throw these scum out of the Helvyndelve."

"You know that saying, Power corrupts?" grumbled Fungus to Haemar.

"But he's only going to get partial Power."

"Then only partly corrupted then."

"Which part?" asked Haemar.

"The brain. It's always the brain. The rest just follows on, really."

Chapter Seven.

As dawn broke (a high C if anyone was recording the event) over the Honister Crags, reflecting interesting patterns in the rippling Mere, to a largely uninterested universe, Uncle Ben relaxed from his stance at the study window of the cottage. The clear gleam of the day meant a lot to him, as he often doubted he would see it. With a song in his heart – speculate for yourselves which one – he looked over at his wife, still asleep on the couch, then cautiously walked across the room and threw open the kitchen door.

The room still held the tension of last night's defeat of the Taxman. Ben walked to the wall cupboard, and opened it, glancing at the design etched on the inside. He withdrew two sticks of incense, and lit them. One he left on the kitchen table, the other he took with him back to the study. Returning to the window, he became alert as he heard the sounds of a horse galloping. Picking up his staff, he peered out of the window to see a cloaked horseman riding hard towards him along the banks of the Mere. As he watched, the horse stumbled and fell. The rider vanished, but a grey/green hawk appeared and beat rapidly towards the cottage. The horse did not rise.

The hawk dove in through the open window, and smacked into the back of the couch, bouncing over the top to land on the floor behind with a loud thump. Erald stuck his head back over the couch, swearing, but flinched back as he realised he was eye to eye with a rudely awakened Grizelda.

"You have got to learn how to land," she told him.

"Sorry. Got any mice?"

"Mice?"

"Got an appetite after flying like that. Could use a drink instead."

"Here," said Ben, handing him a glass.

"What's this got in it?" Erald asked, after tasting the liquid.

"Water."

"Well take it away and put something else in it. Do you know what's been going on?"

Ben pointed to a stack of weapons in a corner, which contravened a number of Local Authority Strategic Arms Treaties and Planning Conditions. "After the Taxman, I had a few visitors last night. Bit of Balefire sent them off, though. They left this lot behind."

"The Helvyndelve!" gasped Erald.

"What of it?" asked Grizelda, with a dangerous tone in her voice.

"Surdin! Bodgandor led by a local wizard have stormed the Delve, and fight under Swirral Edge and Lower Man. The Northern Delve is wholly lost already."

"My niece and nephew are there!"

"Were they with Lord Lakin?"

"Dunno," said Ben, "they left here with that Fungus."

"I will go to see what aid I can give, but there are small gangs of Bodgandor roaming the valley. Ill Luck for any human who meets them!"

"We got two horses here, so I'm coming wi' yer."

"What about me?" asked Grizelda angrily.

"You are needed here, and you know it. This is where they will come if they escape from the Delve. I'll let you know as soon as I can that they are safe if I find them first..."

"Their mother has a wicked tongue on her," warned Grizelda.

The two men, knowing that Grizelda was an expert here, treated this observation with great respect.

"So make sure you bring them back safe."

Moments later, two horses were ridden fiercely out of the cottage grounds, and towards the fells.

"The Bowder Stone entrance is still clear, but it will be watched," observed Erald.

"Look! Dale Head is no longer manned (dwarfed). The scouts have been withdrawn." He looked grim.

"If they are fighting in the Central Delve," asked Ben, "how will we get inside now?"

"The Western Delve exits will be clear, and if they have not sealed the ways in, I can gain admittance."

They spoke no more, but as they passed the bridge where the children had met Lakin, a raven landed on Erald's shoulder (and relieved itself in relief) then spoke into his ear. Erald turned to Ben in disbelief. "They have taken the Council Chamber. The

Steward has been killed, so has Lord Helmar. They got as far as the Chamber of the Throne before being driven back. The Northern and Southern Delves are lost. I can scarce believe it!"

Crows gathered above them as they rode now, like an unpleasant cloud. At the end of the valley stood another bridge, this openly held by a file of Bodgandor. Erald raised his hand and shouted: lightening fell about the bridge, and the Bodgandor fled.

"I am glad you are good at dealing with files," said Ben. "I hate paperwork."

"They will attack again, before we leave the Road."

Erald was right. Round the next corner, a tree lay across the road. Uncle Ben pointed his staff, and the tree exploded into a cloud of splinters, driving the Bodgandor back. Arrows fell around them, but the horsemen burst through the cloud and carried on.

"That's not too ecologically sound," Erald grumbled.

"Nonsense. What's left will go on someone's garden an' keep the weeds down."

"That lot will never clear it up though."

Then the conversation flagged as the crows descended onto them. Erald cut at the birds with his sword and Ben yelled curses at them, before they pulled off the road into the trees. Driven off by the bad language (and the branches) the crows pulled away. Ben and Erald dismounted, and walked deeper into the trees, to find the Bowder Stone, high on the slopes of King How. The atmosphere was as tense as a dentist's waiting room. At the tree line, they stopped.

"They are probably hiding in the old fort behind Castle Crags. No wonder Dale Head was abandoned." Erald observed, observantly.

"How can you tell?"

"I can see things that are hidden, you know."

"Missed us though," came a voice just behind them.

"Who said that?" asked Erald, stopping.

"We did." Two dwarfs with drawn swords stood behind them.

"Why do you seek the Hidden Doors with such haste?" One of the dwarfs enquired.

"With half Caer Surdin roamin' on the hills, wouldn't you be in a hurry?"

"We are not taking risks at the moment."

"Me, you know," said Erald, still scanning the fell around them. "What are your names?"

"As we have seen you before, in the Delve and in friendship, we will tell."

"Go on then."

"Don't tell him, Daran. Whoops."

"Oh good grief, Milim. Can't you do anything right?"

"Did think I made a mistake once, but I was wrong."

"I could see that."

"Mind you…"

"What?"

"Some mistakes are too good to be a one off."

"Will you two stop wittering, and let us in?" asked Erald, whilst Ben just shook his head.

Below them on the hillside, came a bellow of rage.

"We have been seen," remarked Erald.

On seeing the Bodgandor emerge from the tree line below them, the dwarfs stopped bickering. Why waste a good argument when you can come back to it at a better time? Hastily all four dragged the protesting horses around the back of the Bowder Stone, and through the gaping Doors into Helvyndelve. The Doors slammed shut behind them. Inside the Helvyndelve, spluttering, fitful torches lighted the entry cave.

"What happened to the lights?" asked Erald.

"They have taken the Great Deep, and the power is erratic."

"Like the mains Electric then," muttered Ben.

"Most of the garrison here have gone to join the fight, and we were the last patrol out before the Doors here are to be Sealed. Now we fight to hold the Western Passage, and the Bodgandor will not pass our Doors here. But much of the Helvyndelve is in the hands of our enemies."

"Do you know where Lord Lakin is?" asked Erald.

"We heard he was in the fighting at the Chamber of the Throne."

"Two children of men were with him."

"And are still as far as we know. Who are they?"

"Relatives of Grizelda."

"Cor, you wouldn't want to get on the wrong side of her."

Ben's brow darkened, and the dwarfs took the hint.

"Least, that's what we heard. Don't know her myself; sure she's a lovely witch – human-person when you get to know her. Do you know her?"

"I'm married to her."

The dwarfs' expressions indicated respect. (And sympathy, of course, with a bit of admiration thrown in.)

"And yer right. Yer don't wanna get on the wrong side of her, believe me."

Ben leant towards the horrified dwarfs. "The last one who did, she cursed."

"What did she do?"

Ben looked critically at the two dwarfs. "Nah, you aint old enough to be told."

"But I'm three hundred and fifty!"

"Years or waist size?"

"Years."

"Then you've waisted them."

An armoured dwarf bowed in front of them, the joints in his mail slipping easily in tribute to the powers of WD-40. "I am Edchern, and am to lead the last detachment going East to the fighting. Would you wish to be with our party?"

"Do we get ice cream and jelly?"

"No!"

"Good, then I'm with you."

Ben and Erald joined the group of dwarfs setting off along the Passage.

"Do you need weapons?" asked Edchern.

"We already carry what we need," replied Erald.

From time to time, as they passed along the Passage they came across great pools of light. In each stood an armoured dwarf, who rang a hand bell at intervals. Neither Erald nor Ben needed telling that if the bells fell silent, the Bodgandor had arrived.

Some time passed in silence, then Ben said, softly, "The Helvyndelve is greater than I had imagined. Now, I regret that I did not come here earlier, when all the lamps were lit and the carvings clear to be seen."

"The lamps were beyond imagining, and the great caverns of the Deeps were astonishing," replied Erald. "But the carvings were mainly graffiti, and usually obscene."

"Still sorry I missed them, then."

Ben called to the Leader. "Edchern, I feel the breath of a cold power shivering in the air."

"You feel the Power of the Amulet of Kings. It reflects the nature of he who wields The Amulet, and our leaders have had cold natures these last centuries."

"Course, really they were too mean to run the heating," said his Deputy.

On down the Passage they walked, until a dwarf in a Guard Cell stopped them. "From here, ready your weapons," he advised. "This is where they reached, before we threw them back." They entered a round chamber, from which several tunnels led in many directions. Each tunnel had a complement of fiercely armed dwarfs stationed there.

"They still send companies down that Way," he pointed to a dark shaft that led deep into the heart of the Delve, "But we see to it that they do not return."

One large, and ornately carved arch led to a large cavern. Ben and Erald were pushed into this, and motioned to keep quiet. The dwarves drew back into shadows, as a troop of Bodgandor trotted warily up the passage and into the round meeting chamber. Their leader pulled out what seemed to be a map, and headed down the Western Passage. Two parties of dwarfs slipped out of the shadows and followed them.

"That's seen the back of them," said Edchern, cheerfully.

"Well, yes. They walked away from us, so what else would we look at?"

Daran tapped Erald on the arm. "Leader meant, that we wouldn't see them again."

"Probably cos they'll get lost in the dark, eh?"

"Right, Milim."

The dwarfs, Erald and Ben walked into the Grand Cavern. Ben looked around in astonishment at the sheer size of the cavern. It was larger than a Railway Station, and smelt very similar to the toilets.

Erald pulled a face. "You dwarfs are impatient aren't you?"

"How can you tell that?"

"Bet you get caught short a lot."

"We've always been short."

"And hard when caught."

"That's the chain mail."

"Look!" cried Ben.

Up the broad stairs into the far end of the cavern came a disciplined group of dwarfs, surrounded by a baying mob of Bodgandor, who were making a lot of noise but staying out of reach of the dwarfs' short swords (what other kind would they carry?).

At once the rest of the dwarfs in the cavern yelled out in reassurance: "We'll be there shortly!" and charged to the rescue. The Bodgandor paused only long enough to throw a volley of spears at the advancing lines of dwarfs before turning and running back down the stairs.

Erald grabbed the nearest newly arrived dwarf to question him: "What's going on?"

"We are the guard of the Lord Lakin, come from the Chamber of the Throne."

"Where is he then?"

"Dunno. A Troll managed to get into the Chamber of the Throne, and forced the Doors wide. This horde of Bodgandor attacked us, and there were so many we had to retreat. I fear that the Chamber of the Throne has fallen to them, for whilst they will not fight as fiercely as we will there are so many of them that we were overwhelmed."

Erald was underwhelmed at the news. "And where is Lord Lakin?"

"Dunno. We were swept apart in the struggle. We last saw him, with others and the two menchildren with the magic amulets near the dais, but they could not get near enough to join us as we forced our way out."

"What's happened to them then?" Ben asked urgently.

"We do not know, but they were close to Lord Lakin, and they could have tried for the Secret Passages behind the Dais after the Dark Wizard seized the Amulet of Kings."

"What Amulet?" asked Erald.

"What Secret Passage?" asked Ben.

The dwarf looked from one to the other, unsure who to answer first.

"What Amulet?" asked Erald

"What Secret Passage?" asked Ben.

The dwarf's head swung back and forth between the two.

"What Amulet?" asked Erald.

The dwarf's head swung back again, but his helmet kept going until the back of it covered his face. "Mmmmmm," came the muffled reply.

Ben grabbed the dwarf's helmet and twisted it round until his face reappeared. The view was not improved.

"The Wizard found the lost Amulet of Kings behind the dais. The secret passages are, of course, secret. Can you keep a secret?"

"Yes," said Ben.

"So can I." The dwarf stomped off in a huff.

"If Surdin have the Amulet, that's serious!" exclaimed Erald.

"Not as serious as losing the kids. Fighting a horde of maddened Bodgandor would be a breeze compared to dealing with Dot."

"So what do you suggest?" asked Erald.

"Duck."

"Roasted? Will that work?"

"No, DUCK!" Ben pulled Erald down, just as a storm of arrows flew across the Cavern from a troop of Bodgandor gathering at the top of the stairs. They crouched down near the entry arch, whilst the enraged dwarfs gathered themselves together to attack the archers.

"Listen." hissed Ben. "I know that Ned, he's greedy. That's how Surdin got hold of him in the first place."

"Would he want the roast duck?"

"Don't be silly. What he wants is Power, and the Amulet can give it to him."

"Right. But he will have to get a measure of control over it first."

"So, being a sneak, he will sneak off with it. He will need to get some spirits first."

"So, we could trap him in the pub?"

"Nah, better at the Stone Circle. He will need that place to attune to the Power of the Amulet. But how do we find out that Linda and Chris are safe?"

"How can they be safer here than being with Lakin? If he has led them into the secret places of the dwarfs, then we are not going to find them. So let's concentrate on Ned."

"Suppose that makes sense. Erald. But how are we going to get out of this battle to do that?"

"Like this." Erald strode out into the Cavern.

"Oh, no," groaned Ben. "He's going to try something stupid, I can just see it."

Erald justified that suspicion, by pushing dwarfs aside until he could see the Bodgandor who were clustered by the stairs leading to the Chamber of the Throne.

"I speak to the Slaves of Surdin!" Erald called in a vast voice, which filled the Cavern.

"Ere," Milim asked generally. "Aint this fraternisation with the enemy? Is he just allowed to go off and speak to them like that?"

"Why not? He always speaks to us like that," answered Edchern.

"Do you mean us?" A huge Bodgandor stopped leaning on the wall and shook itself all over, a bit like a wet shaggy dog, but without the hair loss.

"I am of the Tuatha. You all fear me, for I have the Power. I shake the trees in the Storm, mine is the Power to lose the Winds!"

"Bet he's been eating those beans again," muttered Daran. "Give me awful wind."

Erald threw up his arms, and began to chant a spell at the unimpressed Bodgandor. But before he could complete the incantation, a shaft of red light flew up the stairs, and turned into a column of fire, which shrank into a spiral of flame.

"Pretty effect," observed Ben, who now grabbed his staff and walked towards Erald who stood silent now, facing the flames which gradually cooled, and turned into a glowing Troll, holding a blood-red sword in one hand, and a ceramic staff in the other.

"Stay here," said the Troll, "and I will turn your spine into a flute, that you may dance in endless pain to the music."

"Can't play proper music with a flute," answered Erald

"He's right there," commented Ben, drawing closer.

"Jethro Tull managed, so I'll have a good go," warned the FireTroll.

"You're just living in the past there. Besides, the witches promised me protection against that spell, so try again."

"Don't bandy words with me."

"I wouldn't say that with legs like yours, if I was you."

"Your insults mean nothing to me."

"I can try harder."

"Know that I am a FireTroll, bathed in the Flames of Caer Surdin."

"I am of the Tuatha, and hold the power of Wind and Rain."

The FireTroll just laughed. The laughter rang round the chamber, and the red troll seemed to glow, and grow. Heat rolled from its body in waves, and the dwarfs and Bodgandor gasped as the temperature rose higher. Neither Erald nor Ben seemed overly impressed however. Raising its sword, the FireTroll spun round, and again flared into a pillar of flame. The cavern became hotter still, with many armoured dwarfs falling to their knees and panting for breath. Pointing its sword, the FireTroll sent a shaft of flame roiling across the cavern towards the two. Dismissively, Erald raised his staff, and the flames flickered past him and went out.

"You could have waited," grumbled Ben, from just behind Erald.

"Didn't have a chance to light me pipe from it."

"Sorry. I'll remember next time."

The FireTroll was less impressed, particularly by the repartee. "You will wish your bones to Ash!"

"Didn't like them," Ben answered.

"Who?" asked Erald, confused.

"Wishbone Ash. All that synthetic stuff."

"You mean synthesiser."

"Do I?"

"Yes."

"Wasn't keen on them, either."

"Do not jest with me," interrupted the FireTroll, who also was not keen on prog rock. "I will light a fire in your bones, whilst living inside your body, and you will scream in the agony!"

"He should try livin with Grizelda for a few weeks. He'd soon learn some manners then. An' listen up, you!" Ben addressed the FireTroll: "I hear worse threats than that every time I'm late back from the Pub, so if you want to scare me, you'll have to put some effort in."

The FireTroll swirled its staff, and then banged in hard down on the rock floor. Bits flew off the end of the staff, which then cracked. The bottom third fell off.

"Don't you just hate it when that happens," Ben remarked to Erald, in a conversational tone.

"Yeah. I broke one last year. Embarrassing it can be. Look, he's gone quite red again."

"Could be anger, rather than shame."

"Where did you get it made?" Erald asked the FireTroll, who was staring in disbelief at the staff.

The FireTroll turned the staff over and over in his hands, looking for the makers mark. "Says here: Crafted by The Ancient Mages of Aswan (Egypt) Limited to the design of Caer Surdin, copyright 1150AD. Oh, hang on, there's small bit under that. Made in China."

"Ah," said Ben, knowledgeably. "Cheap modern copy. No wonder it broke when you needed it."

"Wasn't that cheap, either," complained the FireTroll, bitterly.

"They never are."

"Might have been an honest mistake. Maybe the instructions said to bake at so many degrees Fahrenheit, and being foreign, the makers used Centigrade. Overcooked it." Erald mused.

"Not their fault. I suppose they couldn't help being born foreign."

"Better check that sword, too," advised Erald.

The FireTroll dropped the broken staff, and kicked it away in disgust, rather harder than he had intended. There was a brief scream, as the remains impaled a Bodgandor who had been in the line of fire.

"It were good for something, anyway," Ben said to Erald.

"Bit expensive as a spear though."

The FireTroll examined the sword carefully. "This one should be OK. It's been in my family for generations. Let's see if it works, shall we?" The FireTroll swung the sword viciously at Erald, who stepped back, smartly. "That worked well," the FireTroll smirked.

Erald sneered back. "Unambitious."

"Let's see now." The FireTroll muttered to himself, then swirled the sword in a pattern, and pointed it at a dwarf who was examining the remains of the staff and the Bodgandor impaled on it. The dwarf yelled, and then went very quiet, and fell over. Steam rose from its armour.

"An acquired taste, a bit like Lobster," observed the FireTroll. "Cooked the same way, too. In the shell. So, now we know that this works. Multi function, see?"

Ben raised his staff, and strode forward.

"What's this, a job lot?" sneered the FireTroll, and the sword again spurted flame.

But Ben spun his staff in front of him, a blur in his hands, and the flames scattered harmlessly.

"Who taught you that, Robin Hood?"

"Astonishing what you can pick up around the place."

"Bet you learnt that from him too."

With a wild yell, the FireTroll jumped forward swinging the sword, only to step on the broken end of its staff, which rolled away, taking the FireTroll's left foot with it. Ben stepped forward promptly, and shoved forward with his staff. The FireTroll fell backwards and lay there, dazed. In dismay, the Bodgandor turned, and ran back down the stairs. Ben and Erald grabbed the FireTroll, which had lost his heat for battle, and so had cooled down, and pulled him the short distance to the top of the stairs.

"That's far enough," panted Erald.

"Too much like hard work," agreed Ben.

"Hard Work never killed anyone."

"Why take the chance?"

The FireTroll shook his head, to clear it, and sat up. Ben and Erald backed away. "What did you two clowns do to me?"

"Us?"

"Where's my Staff?"

"What do you remember?"

"Coming up the stairs here, and listenin' to you two make bad jokes."

"Well, maybe you did not bring it."

"That might explain why you are still alive."

"What could a FireTroll like you do to us?"

"Not telling. It would give you nightmares."

The FireTroll shook his head, and glared at Erald. "Stay here. I'm coming back for you."

"When you've got your Staff?"

"Right."

The FireTroll raised its sword, and made some mystic passes. A flaming red rune appeared in the air at the top of the stairs, and hung there glowing as the troll turned, and lumbered slowly down the stairs and out of sight. Ben and Erald turned away, just as the FireTroll's head reappeared at the top of the stairs (the rest of the troll was still attached, just out of sight). "I'll be back."

"Isn't it illegal to say that unless you are wearing sunglasses?"

But the troll really had gone this time.

Erald turned to his companion. "Give me your staff."

"Not a chance."

"Oh, all right then. Where's Edchern?"

"Here!" called the dwarf, approaching cautiously.

"Pass me one of your spears."

"Here you go."

Erald grabbed the spear, winced, and moved his grip from the sharp bit on the end with which all spears are traditionally equipped. He then carefully prodded the rune-sign with the end of the spear. There was a flash of light, and the whole spear crumbled into ashes in his hand. With a small curse he dropped the (now very hot) spear tip.

"That was my favourite spear!" said Edchern.

"Well, he did that right, anyway," Erald said, grudgingly.

"What is it?" asked the dwarf.

"The rune-sign Terilan. See, you cannot get to the head of the stairs without touching the sign, and if you did, you would meet the same fate as that spear."

"So the Troll has sealed away that part of the Helvyndelve from us?"

"Basically, yes. But the Bodgandor cannot pass it either, so you cannot be assaulted from there, and this cavern is safe now for a while, as is the Western Passage. But Lord Lakin and Grizelda's wards are on the wrong side of the rune-sign."

"Can you put it out?"

Erald thought for a moment, then raised his arms and chanted briefly: a shower of water poured out of the end of his staff onto the glowing rune-sign, which hissed, crackled and spat like a demented breakfast cereal. But failed to go out. The water flow ran out to a dribble, and then ceased.

"That will be a 'No' then?" asked Edchern.

"We will retire, to think. Post a couple of Guards and we will confer." Erald drew Ben away from the (now slightly smug) glowing rune-sign to a corner of the cavern.

"Have you come across this before?" Erald muttered.

"No. I do not normally deal with this stuff, I'm better with the goats, really."

"You got away from the FireTroll's attack."

"Livin' with Grizelda, I have to be *really good* at the defensive stuff. But she doesn't normally throw things like that at me. The water spell didn't work. How about ice?"

"Ice?"

"Ice. Freeze it out."

"Let's work on it. After all, that's a defensive spell so it must be possible to break it."

Chapter Eight

The FireTroll stumbled back into the Chamber of the Throne, and found Ned taking his ease in the Throne, studying the Amulet.

"What happened to you?" asked the sorcerer, dropping his aitch but not looking very hard for it.

"Not sure really. I'm a bit dazed and confused," confessed the FireTroll.

"I didn't bargain for you."

"What?"

"Forget it. That shouldn't be hard in your state."

The Troll dropped to the floor at the foot of the dais. "What are you doing?" he asked.

"Trying to get my head round this Amulet. Even for me…"

(The Troll snorted derisively. Its sarcasm function had not been impaired.)

"The Amulet remains a subtle challenge. It is ancient, and not easily controlled."

"Bit like the Duke of Edinburgh, then. So what are you thinking? The Grey Mage?"

"I would prefer to be in charge of this meself."

"Right. So, the plan is?"

"I'm thinking that we need to get to a Place of Power."

"I'm not keen on leaving here with those two running about."

"Which two?"

"That Tuatha, and him who lives with the witch on the lakeside."

"You didn't just leave them there?"

"Nah, left a rune-sign at the top of the stairs. They'll not get through that, so don't worry about a bunch of dwarfs suddenly running down the stairs and taking you by surprise."

"Wasn't worried about that."

"No?" The Troll grinned, nastily. He was returning to normal.

"Hey, have you seen my staff anywhere?"

"No. Thought yer had it with you. Anyway, how come they got in the Helvyndelve?"

"Cursed Bodgandor at the Bowder Stone didn't move fast enough to stop them. Mind you, when I'm myself again I intend to have a bit of fun with them."

The FireTroll stood up, and walked up to the Throne. He peered at the Amulet. "Fancy looking thing. Is it all its made out to be?"

"It is the most powerful thing round here."

"How much competition has it got?"

The troll thought for a moment. "Well, let's see if you can get on top of this before all Caer Rigor descends on us to get it back."

"Yer probably right. There's a Place of Power just above the Northern Delve. Who's goin' to look after things whilst we go there?" asked Ned.

"There's those three RockTrolls knocking about, and the Bodgandor you let loose in the tunnels."

"They will have to do. This place is Ok, a bit dusty, but this Amulet's what we came for. Those teenage kids are about somewhere with the Wards, but there's not much they can do. So I reckon we'll stay in charge."

"We've never been in charge. That's the Grey Mage, and you'd do well not to forget it. If he comes down here with a couple of my brothers, you are in real trouble."

"Me? Not We?"

"'We' all you want."

"Don't be rude."

"If Surdin, no *when* Surdin, arrive to see what you've managed to do, if you've got that trinket and not told them, *you* are in real trouble. Be nothing to do with me. So there's no we in it. Except for what you do in your pants."

"Best we get on then. We'll use the Calfhow Pike exit." Ned stood up, and he and the Troll walked towards the North Door. As an afterthought, Ned beckoned to a small troop of Bodgandor resting near the North Door, and told them to follow him. They passed through the Doors and hurried into the darkened Northern Delve, the Bodgandor at their heels.

*

The heavy door swung shut behind the small party of dwarfs and the others of course, and at once all the light went out. The tiny, now very cramped passage was now lit only by the faint glow from Fungus. Linda was scared, and Chris very nervous, but the dwarfs all seemed completely at home. The sound of the fighting was also cut off by the closing door, and Lakin seemed more alarmed by that.

"I hope that we are not losing the Chamber of the Throne to them," he worried.

"Well, we had to take refuge here," said Haemar, practically.

"Yes, because we was cut off," added another dwarf.

"I think I had something cut off," complained a second dwarf.

"Shame it wasn't your tongue, then."

"That's not very nice."

"Like you then."

"Settle down," ordered Lakin. "We're all in this together, so we are gonna make the best of it. Right?"

There was a lot of mumbling along the lines of "if we must" "oh, OK then" "I will if he will…"

Fungus shook his head. "Dwarfs. Here we are, in a right mess, an all they can do is moan."

"We can do lots of other things, too," said a dwarf who was clearly struggling with his anger management.

"I said leave it out!" exclaimed Lakin.

"Where are we?" asked Linda, with a tremor in her voice.

"This," Lakin explained to her (and in fact to Fungus and most of the dwarfs as well), "is one of the secret tunnels of the Helvyndelve." He obviously expected this to be greeted with astonishment, but all he got back was general agreement.

"Right."

"Thought it must be that."

"Didn't know it was there."

"Because it was a secret? Right?"

"Right!"

"Good secret, when we didn't know it was there, and we must have made it!"

"I didn't make it."

"Only thing you ever made was a mess."

"At least I made something, not like you."

"Shut up and listen to me," Lakin ordered.

"Now, these are the Secret Tunnels of the Helvyndelve. Not all were made by the dwarfs, and only those of the Blood Royal know the entrances and routes through them. These tunnels are numerous, and they branch out in many strange directions.

But I know, for I was taught, some of the routes through them. So stay with me, do not wander off, for in these places, all those who wander get lost."

At a sign from Lakin (actually, he pointed and then bopped the nearest dwarf hard on the helmet to ensure he had got his point across) the dwarfs picked up several torches that lay on the ground nearby, and with only a slight singing of beards managed to light them. The faint glow revealed a narrow tunnel, about three dwarfs wide and five feet high, with rough sides and an uneven floor. Fungus had already been pushed someway down the tunnel by the pressure of dwarfish bodies and the two teenagers, and was looking nervous.

"Fungus, I thought that you were at home underground," said Chris.

"Well, yes, but these tunnels are a bit uncanny, you know? And it's a while since I had a drink."

"Alcohol is no cure for problems you know," Linda scolded him.

"No, but if you drink enough, the problem goes away. Anyway, I thought you were supposed to be homesick?"

"Funny. I was," replied Linda, "but since that fight it seems to have gone away."

"It's in her genes," said Haemar.

"Her Levis?" asked Chris.

"No, her genes. Yours too, I suppose. Just look at Grizelda, yer aunt. No one here would want to get into a scrap with her. And Linda's goin' the same way."

Lakin pushed past them, keeping the blazing torch in his hand a safe distance from his beard. "Follow me!" he growled, and headed off into the dark. The tunnel rose steeply, twisting up over the roof of the Chamber of the Throne, and then falling back to the level of the floor. The small party cursed constantly at the rough flooring and badly cut steps, the dwarfs offering professional criticism.

"Who cut these then? A blind, drunken idiot on his first day at work?"

"Or just an idiot blind drunk?"

"Either would make a better job than you could."

"Quiet," ordered Lakin. "Honestly, I would have been better bringing Fungus' Band than you lot."

"Um," remarked Scar.

"Is this the time to tell him?" asked Felldyke, sotto voice.

"He's going to find out anyway," said Haemar.

"Oh no. Don't tell me," groaned Lakin. "Instead of my picked selection of ruthless killers, I came in here with…"

"The Banned Underground."

"To be fair," said Haemar quickly. "Scar can be pretty vicious if he's roused."

"What does it need to rouse him? A couple of million volts?"

"Try giving him lager by mistake."

"Very useful. I must remember to carry some, in case we get

into a fight."

"Lord, there are some of us here."

"How many exactly?"

"Er, six of us."

"*Six?* What happened to the rest of you?"

"Someone shut the door to the passage."

"So?"

"Well, being a secret, none of the rest knew how to get in, did they?"

"Great. Just Great. What are we going to do if we get into a fight?"

"Rely on the Power of Music?"

"Not very helpful, Fungus. Oh well, we'll just have to make the best of it."

Lakin turned, and moodily trudged off along the tunnel, kicking at a loose stone as he went (he would have been very happy to see the stone bounce of the wall, and fly back to hit Haemar on the nose. But it was dark, so he didn't.)

"Ow. Something hit me on the nose."

"Wasn't me."

"I know that, Scar."

"How? Could've been me!"

"Because you are behind me."

"Oh. Right."

"Quiet now," hissed Lakin. "We are beside the Throne." He carefully pulled a heavy curtain aside, dislodging enough dust to fill the corridor to waist level The curtain then disintegrated, to the annoyance of a family of large spiders, who had lived there for uncounted generations. Well, spiders can only count to eight, so they had stopped counting after that. Lakin then peered cautiously through the two small holes that appeared in the wall. He could see the FireTroll standing close to Ned, who was lounging on the Throne. He moved, and placed his ear to the hole, and listened for a while. Then his face set.

"What's wrong?" asked Linda, with concern.

"Spider just bit my ear!" Lakin dropped the remains of the curtain, and the new dust storm completely enveloped Felldyke. The band members combined to pull him out.

"Now I know their plan," announced Lakin. "They plan to take the Amulet of Kings to a Place of Power, there to attune Ned to the Amulet that he may access its Power."

Again he was disappointed, as no cries of amazement followed this. Well, Felldyke cried in amazement, but that was only because his head had been dug out from the sea of dust in which he was buried.

"Erald and your Uncle," here he nodded at the two children, "have fought and beaten a FireTroll, but the FireTroll has sealed the stairs to the upper levels and the Western Passage, so we can get no help from there."

"How did Uncle Ben get in here?" asked Chris in surprise.

"Probably followed you two. If we weren't in this war, we could put a revolving door in instead of the Ancient and Magical ones we are lumbered with at the moment."

"There's some good ones at B & Q," advised Fungus. "Cheap too."

"No."

"Won't last long."

"Nothing seems to last for long down here, except for the dust."

"Shut up, Haemar."

"Lakin," asked Linda, "where is this Place of Power?"

"Well, there are a few about. But the nearest is the one that they will head for, as Ned plans to double cross his boss, the Grey Mage."

"I thought he was off with the others in France, at that conference."

"So did I, Fungus, but maybe he finished his holiday early."

"I can understand that," agreed Haemar. "I went to France once." He shuddered at the memory.

"Just once?"

"Some mistakes you make again, because they were good fun. Not that one."

"Right."

"So," said Linda, persistently: "where is the place?"

"She can't be hungry again. Not at a time like this."

"I think, Haemar, she meant *place*, not *plaice.*"

"Well, how am I supposed to tell if it is not written down?"

"Con text."

"Sounds like a con trick."

Not for the first time, Lakin chose to ignore them. "The nearest Place of Power will be the Stone Circle above Castlerigg. The way is long from the Northern delve, but shorter for us from the Western Passage. But that is the closest Place he will know, so Ned will go there. Maybe if we can get there first, we can recover the Amulet from him. Friends, who will journey with me?"

"He's the only one who knows the way out, right?"

"That's right, Scar."

"Then I'm with you."

"Me too!"

"And me."

"Well," said Fungus, "looks like you've got us all, Lakin."

"Excellent. Willing volunteers." Lakin looked carefully around at this band of volunteers, then laughed, rather sardonically and led them off down the narrow passage, the burning torch sending sparks into his beard. (He occasionally paused, causing some congestion and ruffled tempers behind him, to put them out.) The tunnels remained rough hewn, and twisted and turned in all directions. Some small side passages opened out, but Lakin ignored most of them. Until he reached one low opening, which was even dingier than the others. Here he motioned all to be very quiet, and they stole past the ill-formed archway. Chris, feeling brave, stopped to investigate.

"Hey!" he whispered, urgently. "I can hear something!"

Linda joined him at the mouth of the tunnel. "There's a lot of splashing noises."

"Listen, there's a voice."

Faintly they heard an echo: "We hates him! We hates him forever!"

Fungus stooped to listen as well, then straightened up so fast his glasses fell off. He bent down to get them back, and banged his head on the wall of the passage. "That's never him!" he said to Lakin in surprise.

"Yes, it is, I am afraid. Sad really."

"Who – or what – is it?" asked Linda.

"Gormless Golem we call him. See, he thought music would be better with electronics all over it. Progress he called it. But Lord Lucan, well he was a traditionalist, and didn't agree. So he made him come and live in here, where he hoped none of it would leak out. Gormless has been in here ever since."

"We'd all forgotten him, really," added Haemar.

"Come on quick, if he hears us – especially Fungus – he'll go mad."

"Why?" asked Linda, treating Fungus to a glare.

Fungus did not feel so treated by being glared at. "He was very strange. He hated jazz."

"I'm not entirely sure that qualifies him as being strange," said Chris.

The Banned Underground looked at Chris as if *he* was strange.

"Better leave him here with him," suggested Felldyke, whose intentions were clearer than his syntax. Typical drummer.

"Nah," objected Haemar. "That would be a cruel and unusual punishment. For Gormless."

"Oi! I heard that," objected Chris.

"Come on," ordered Lakin, and they trooped off into the darkness, whilst the wails and strange noises carried on behind them. The long march seemed to last forever. Lakin was in front, muttering now into his beard. Linda wanted to start talking to him, but one of the guards stopped her.

"He mutters to recite the way. Do not disturb him, lest he becomes lost – and we do not get out."

Linda nodded.

"It is a Long March, this," said Haemar.

"Didn't you realise that it's July?"

"What's that got to do with how far we've walked?"

The conversation petered out as the tunnel walls now closed in, and the party had to walk in single file. The roof closed down, and Chris had to stoop as he walked. The torches burned less fiercely, and the light began to fade. Linda was getting nervous again.

"Don't worry, Linda," Lakin reassured her. "In a moment we will come to a higher chamber, where we may rest."

Indeed, he was right, for shortly after the roof rose to a high ceiling, the walls spread out, and they entered a chamber equipped with stone seats and a welcome supply of fresh torches. "Here," Lakin explained, we are under the slopes of Seat Sandel. We may rest here in safety, and take some ease."

Several of the dwarfs still had their backpacks, and they distributed drinks round the group. After the guards had surrounded Fungus and talked quietly to him for a moment, his pack also revealed a large supply of Kendal Mint Cake. This was a welcome find for the teenagers; particularly Linda who tended to get ratty if left unfed for too long.

"How come you had lots of this stuff, then, Fungus?" asked Chris.

Fungus looked around, shiftily. "Thing is, for us BogTrolls, that's a legal high. Gives us a real fizz, you know?"

"What do you want it for then?"

"Well, sometimes it's hard, gigging a lot. Takes it out of you, and you just need a pick me up. That stuff works for me."

"And we thought you did drugs."

"Well now you know: but keep it quiet eh? Got a reputation to keep, I have. Punters prefer their musicians to be stoned."

"I thought that was only if you played badly?"

"I never play badly, man."

Linda had other things on her mind, and was looking round the cavern thoughtfully. She stared at a group of three dwarfs near a wall. Steam rose about their feet. "Fungus, can you see an alcove or something?"

"Why?"

"Can't you guess?"

"Ah. Well, there isn't one, really."

"Do you have to?" asked Chris, wearily.

"When you gotta go, you gotta go."

"Then go in the passage we just left. But don't go too far down it," said Fungus.

Linda stood up, and walked back into the passageway.

"Girls," muttered Chris, then went to join the group of dwarfs.

Linda's scream echoed round the cavern. A moment later, the dwarfs were running hard towards the sound.

"Just shows." Fungus observed. "If dwarfs were clear thinkers, they would run *away* from screams, not towards them."

Chris was not amused. "That's my sister screaming."

"Then why are you not running towards her?"

"Don't want to get in their way."

And indeed, the dwarfs did look very warlike with their swords and shields at the ready. Linda backed quickly out of the passageway, and stopped when one sharp sword poked her in the bum. "Ow!"

"Sorry."

"Why did you yell like that?" Lakin asked, getting to the bottom of the matter. "And what on earth were you doing in there on your own? I told you not to wander off!"

"Well, I needed a pee, and then I heard heavy breathing."

"We don't get that sort of voyeur down here."

"Dwarves are less exotic than that," put in Fungus.

"Haemar. You and a couple of others go twenty yards down there and check it out," muttered Lakin. The dwarfs left, quiet as only a dwarf underground can be. A moment later they returned, dragging a dwarf sized, but very thin, figure.

"It was only Gormless," announced Haemar.

"Name fits him perfectly," sulked Linda.

"About the only thing that still does," remarked Haemar. The dwarf's clothes hung off him in rags: he was very, very thin and looked ill.

"Help me," he breathed.

"Take a good look at him," said Lakin, not without some sympathy for the wretched plight of the dwarf. "Any one else into progressive music?"

"Pity me," pleaded Gormless, miserably. "I will recant and stick to blues and rock n roll now."

"Lord Lucan it was who imprisoned you here. I do not think I have the right to free you."

Fungus, unusually, stuck up for the miserable pleader. "Lucan's gone, and you're the Boss now. Let him come with us."

"Why are you supporting him, Fungus?"

"Old time's sake, I suppose. And he was the only one of you lot ever learnt to bend a guitar note. Without bending the guitar, that is."

The other band members muttered agreement, and even the guards looked a bit sympathetic. "If he's prepared to promise, Lord," said Dalan, a guard with a kindly nature (and hence an anomaly).

"Well, OK. But this is the deal. If there is fighting, you will take your share, Gormless, and stick to your promise. OK?"

"I promise, Lord. Anything to get out of here."

"Break time over," Lakin called. Grabbing a torch, he spun on his heel, but the metal was so shiny that he ended up facing the way he started, and the effect was lost. Fungus started to giggle, but quickly turned it into a cough. Lakin glared at him, and tuned more carefully.

"Follow me!" he ordered, and led the way out of the cavern into another passage. This too was low, and narrow, with roughly hewn walls and floor. The light from the torches was dim and spread out, and many toes were stubbed and elbows banged as the motley cavalcade made its way, muttering, after Lakin. All the torches were burning low by the time Lakin halted at a blank wall. The air in the tunnels was musty, and old, and carried few of the necessities of life and those had gone well past their use by date. That would be the real use by date, not the one put on the packaging to encourage consumers to restock: these consumers were on the verge of exhausting the supply. The two teenagers, for example, were exhausted now and inclined to be rather negative as a result.

"No way out!" complained Chris, loudly.

"What do you mean?" asked Linda, whose belligerence had faded, and she was now entirely fed up of the whole thing and wanted nothing more than to go somewhere peaceful, unenclosed, and enjoy a hot bath, a cold drink, and some cool magazines.

"It's a blank wall, like the Arndale Center."

"But there must be a way out!" Linda was starting to panic a little now.

"Well, there's no way out sign hanging from the ceiling, and pointing to a fire escape."

"Hush," said Lakin, a little wearily. "Of course there is a way out." He unbuckled his sword, took it out of the scabbard, and pushed the scabbard into a small crack in the rock wall. Nothing happened. Lakin took the scabbard out, and rammed it back in, hard. Still nothing happened. Now, Lakin took off his backpack, extracted a small but very heavy hammer, and beat seven bells out of the end of the scabbard.

"Not very catchy," observed Felldyke to Haemar. "Lost the

rhythm a couple of times there."

"I noticed."

"What's he tryin' to do?"

"Open the door, I reckon."

"Why doesn't he turn the handle then?" asked Gormless, from nearby.

"I dunno. Ask him," answered Felldyke.

"Lakin," yelled Haemar, trying to make himself heard over the noise of the hammer.

"What?"

"Gormless says, why don't you turn the handle?"

"What handle?" The hammering stopped, abruptly.

"Clearly leadership material," observed Fungus, gloomily.

"The one that opens the door," offered Gormless, helpfully. The dwarfs next to him restrained themselves (luckily they were a disciplined bunch, because it could not have been easy).

"Where is it then?"

"If you step back four paces and look to your left, there's a small wheel on the wall. Turn it."

Lakin stepped back.

"That was my foot," grumbled Fungus.

On the wall there was a roughly wheel shaped mound of dust.

Lakin shoved the now rather battered scabbard through the wheel, and applied his strength. To no avail. He heaved again on the wheel, straining until his face turned bright red and his language blue.

"Try the other way?" advised Gormless, peering through the dying light of the last torch. Linda let out a small sob. Lakin reversed his efforts, the wheel turned effortlessly, and a very small door opened in the flat end wall of the tunnel. Fresh air [for a given value of fresh] flooded into the tunnel, to the vast relief of all, and the torches were relit. Lakin bent down, as the door was short even for a dwarf, and stuck his head out carefully. He looked each way, and then exited. The others all followed him, with various degrees of difficulty. Fungus kept getting stuck, until he was made to take the sax from his back and push it through separately.

When all were safely out in the wide Passage, Lakin pushed the door shut. As it closed, the outline of the door vanished without trace. Lakin turned to Gormless.

"So how did you know about the wheel then? When I did not?"

"Lord Lucan installed it a few years back, cos he kept using that tunnel as a short cut to avoid people he didn't want to meet. I watched him once, and I've used it myself a few times when there were things I really needed."

"You were imprisoned in there. You were not supposed to go out for a stroll."

"Nah, I know. But I needed guitar strings once in a while, and twice I nipped into town to get some sheet music."

"Well, it was progressive," muttered Fungus.

"You misheard him," advised Haemar. "Gormless said *sheet* music."

"Where are we?" Linda asked Lakin, who was looking up and down the Passage, with concern.

"This is the Western Passage, Linda. But there is no sign of the Guards who should stand at intervals, with lanterns, if the lights are out. Either they got called away to the fighting, or the fighting went past this point. We must keep a good watch now, and be prepared for anything." Lakin told her.

"Carl!" he called softly to one of the guards, "I have heard it said that you have the best eyes in the Delve."

"You want me to lead, Lord?"

"Yes."

"Fine, but I do not know the Western Passage well. I spent most of my time in the Northern Delve."

"Right. Form up," ordered Lakin.

At once, two of the guards joined Carl, and the other three placed themselves at the other end of the group, leaving the Banned Underground in the middle, with Fungus, Chris and Linda. Lakin led them off to the West, keeping to one side of the Passage.

"At least I don't feel like a rat in a drain now," muttered Chris to his sister.

"You still look like one though," she replied.

Chris ignored that sartorial criticism. "Lakin, where exactly are we, and when do we get out?" he asked.

"At the moment, we are in the Western Passage, approaching the Western Delve itself, which I hope is still secure. Shortly, the Passage forks, and we will bear North to leave the Delve, and head for the Place of Power."

"Where exactly is that?"

"You will know it as the stone circle above Castle Rigg."

"But," Linda butted in, "we have been there lots of times and seen nothing."

"Perhaps when you were there, there was nothing to be seen, or else you did not know what it was you were seeing," replied Lakin, cryptically.

"Oh, very gnomic," muttered Fungus.

"Shouldn't that be dwarfic?"

"Doesn't work."

They walked further down the deserted Passage, past several posts which (Lakin told them) should have held guards and lanterns, until Lakin sent Carl on ahead to scout out the way. The party sat down, gratefully, and waited for his return. Shortly, as befitted a dwarf, he did.

"Carl, can you see any of our folk ahead?"

"No, Lord. I went as far as the fork at the Passage Meet, and found no trace of any. But nor was there any sign of a fight. There are no lights, but we may travel on quickly."

"Then let us do so."

Lakin sent two of the six guards down the Passage that led to the Gatehall, and the others marched more swiftly now, down towards the heart of the Western Delve. "See if you can find some food and water," Lakin told the two as they left. "But be quick for we shall not tarry in the Delve."

"That way lies the nearest exit from the Delve, and outside it is evening and the White Lady walks the skies."

"Then let's get out! And get to Aunt Dot's!" exclaimed Linda, but no one else moved, and even Fungus seemed less than keen.

"If the Bodgandor are lose on the slopes, Linda, you would not make it to your aunt's cottage safely," Lakin told her, gently.

"Do you think she will be OK?" Linda asked, with a quiver in her voice.

"Your aunt has more power than a lot of witches realise. She will not play their games, so they discount her strengths, but in a fight she and your Uncle are the ones I would chose to have beside me. Well, in front of me maybe, so that I could see what she was doing, and who she was doing it to."

"And what with," added Fungus, darkly. "I've been in her kitchen." He shuddered.

"What's wrong with her cooking?" asked Linda, defensively. She had decided that she quite liked her aunt.

"You can ask that? When you've eaten there?"

"Be fair, Lakin," Fungus told him, although not very

convincingly. "They did not get to stay there all that long."

"So they never saw the jet propelled goat? The Tethered Pig? Or the Glow in the Dark Free Range Chickens? They must have avoided the herb garden, for heaven's sake. Otherwise they'd glow in the dark, too, like the chickens."

"Why was the pig tethered, Fungus?" asked Felldyke, who shared Linda's interest in food.

"Stop it floating off. Damn thing was the size of a zeppelin, and had as much on board gas. She had tried a spell for a lighter cut of bacon, but got it wrong. Take my advice, and never, *ever,* ask her for a slimming spell. Girl in the village did that, and look what happened to her."

"What?"

"Dunno exactly, but the Council hire her as a lamp post. She didn't like dogs much before that, but you should hear her now."

"So they aren't in any danger, then?" Linda wanted to be sure.

"Not unless the Grey Mage of Surdin were to attack them himself, or Ned if he gains control over the Amulet of Kings."

"Can't you use the Amulet then?" Chris asked Lakin.

"Well I am partly attuned. But the truth is, I do not know if I am strong enough. My Father was fully attuned, and he hardly ever used it. Except when he sang."

"He sang well, your Dad," remembered Haemar.

"No, he was rubbish. But if he wore the Amulet, it gave him

perfect pitch."

"Cor. You could sell that to the record companies, and make a fortune."

"That would be a base use of its Power."

"But, basically, you'd make a shed load of money. And Money = Power. Just ask any of those TV Talent Shows. They'd have the use of it any day, I bet."

"I would not authorise such use. And anyway, I would not permit another to be attuned to the Amulet. What then would become of the Helvyndelve? No, we will seek out Ned, recover the Amulet, and drive these Bodgandor from our home. The Amulet can then clean it all up for us."

"It's pretty clear that they won't do it for themselves," Fungus muttered to Linda.

Lakin walked off down the Passage to the Western Delve, and the others all followed him. And followed him. And followed him. And followed him.

"This tunnel goes on for ever," moaned Fungus.

The rest of the Banned Underground agreed, whilst the dwarf guards stayed silent in respect for their Leader and their feet (not necessarily in that order). Eventually the cavalcade ground to a halt, without seeing another soul on the journey. Linda could not remember ever being so tired. As the grumbles began, Lakin waved them urgently to silence.

"Carl," he hissed: "scout out the way."

The dwarf nodded, and drawing his sword, slid forward into the darkness. Hidden from the others' view, he lit a cigarette, and leant against the wall, blowing a plume of smoke in front of him – only to fall backwards into the dust. He had chosen to lean on an open door, the fate of many who sneak a drag in the dark. Jumping up, he quickly hid the remains of the cigarette, and examined the trails and footsteps in the dust around him. Carefully, he walked into the now open cavern, and examined the guard post, which, like all such places in the universes smelt of cigarettes and boredom. Satisfied that nothing lurked nearby, he left the cavern and returned to the party. He reported to Lakin in a low voice (well, he was a dwarf. Sorry.)

"Dwarfs were here until recently," Carl murmured. "There are no signs of a fight, and they took their weapons with them. There is still some kit, rubbish and food around in the guard room, so it looks as if they went quickly – and with light packs, so they were intending to return."

"I'm coming to take a look," answered Lakin. He went forward to look at the guardroom, and the others all followed. Linda, with a glad cry, jumped on the food set out on the tables around the walls of the guardroom. Felldyke followed her.

"Typical," said Chris, who was under no illusion as to his sister's need for food.

"Well? I'm hungry!"

"But you don't know where that's been."

"Listen, if I told you how much I needed this, I wouldn't have time to eat it."

"Quiet!" hissed Haemar, from the doorway. He had stopped outside, for a personal moment, and so had not joined the others around the guardroom tables.

"Something's coming!"

Lakin grabbed him quickly, and pulled him back into the guardroom. Carl put the torch out, and the guards moved silently to the front with their swords out. The sound of tramping feet could be heard now, and the occasional muffled curse. Haemar pulled Linda back from the doorway to stop her joining the fight.

"Bodgandor," muttered Lakin, and the dwarfs nodded.

The troop of Bodgandor drew nigh, and then stopped. Only three carried torches, and one of those approached the doorway into the cavern. "Can't see anyone, Captain." The Bodgandor had a low, raspy voice.

"Any of our lads here?"

"Can't see anyone, Captain. Just us."

"Rest must be held up, or haven't broken through yet. All right lads, you can stand down."

"Don't you mean sit down? Captain?"

"Sit or stand, do what you want, we might have a bit of a wait until the others get here. I don't fancy searching all these rat holes for a few dwarfs and those men-children all on our own. You never know what might be hiding here."

"Me for example," said Lakin in a loud voice, walking out of the guardroom and lighting his pipe with no thought for the health risk to the teenagers. Behind him, his guards slid silent and unseen out into the passage.

"Who are you then!" demanded the Captain, grabbing his club.

"I am the Lord Lakin, and this is my home."

"Well, you could have cleaned up a bit for our visit."

Lakin spat.

"Bad manners, that," observed the captain.

"Unhygienic," agreed one of his troop.

"What's hygiene?"

"I thought it was just a way of saying hello to someone you knew."

"Who?"

"Gene."

"Idiot."

"I know someone who wants to see you," carried on the Captain, "so you can just come along quietly with us." He waved an arm, and the rest of the Bodgandor scrambled to their feet. All eyes were on Lakin.

"Oh, I think I'll turn that invitation down," he remarked, holding their attention.

"It wasn't an invite, but an order!" The Captain leaped at Lakin, who swung his sword up. The rest of the dwarfs gave a howl, and attacked. Shortly afterwards, they walked back into the guardroom. Each carried a shield blazoned with a red flame on sable.

"Spares in the passage," Lakin remarked easily to the others, and sent Haemar to get enough for all. Haemar came back in again, quickly, and muttered in Lakin's ear.

"Not again. OK, on guard, all of you. A surprise will not be so easy this time!"

"Surprise!" called out two dwarfs, and walked through the doors. The guards sent to the Gatehall had returned, carrying food and water, torches and news. "The garrison at the Gatehall is still in place, though they suffered severe losses when attacked. A new breed of Bodgandor is abroad, carrying shields of sable with a red flame."

"Like unto these?" asked Lakin, pointing at the bodies near the door, and showing the shields taken from the fallen.

The dwarfs looked at each other, and shrugged. "The shields are the same. Anyway, most of the garrison had gone with a Tuatha and a wizard to the Central Delve, where they fought a FireTroll. Those left gave us food, water, torches, and advice."

"Shove off, actually, they said."

"Well, *actually* they said…"

"Children present," Haemar advised them.

"Sorry."

"Right then," said Lakin, decisively. "Onwards." He turned, and led them back through the doorway. "Light as many of the torches as you can," he ordered.

"Linda, Chris, I would like to welcome you both into the Great

Western Cavern.* I wish I could have brought you here when all the lamps were lit, for it is very beautiful."

[* Named for its location, not a sponsorship deal. The attempt to have the place renamed the Virgin Airways Cavern never got off the ground.]

"I've never been here before," said Fungus, a little resentfully.

"Well, this place is Holy to the White Lady, so we do not hold parties or gigs here. No reason for you to come."

"Hey, I can get off on a pretty grotto like anyone else can. Just cos I'm green. Honestly. That's prejudice, that is."

"Realistic though," admitted Haemar.

"It's not easy, being green."

"For us, this place is truly sacred. Strangers nor guests do not come here save with our leave, and that is given rarely."

"Course, all the bloody lamps went out when Lucan lost the Amulet and stopped sending its Power through the Delve," put in Haemar.

"Chris!" exclaimed Linda. "My Ward is glowing!"

"Mine too," replied Chris, pulling the zip down on his jacket, and pulling the chain out to have a look.

"The Wards of Lingard are an Old Magic," said Lakin gravely. "They will respond to the Power of the White Lady, which runs even yet through this place. Try saying 'Luthen' and see what happens."

"Luthen" said Linda and Chris together. At once the Wards filled with a soft, clear light, which spread around the group, illuminating first the ground, and then spreading their radiance more widely. Linda exclaimed in delight at the use of the necklace, whilst even Chris looked around in amazement at the beauty revealed by the light.

"Now" said Lakin earnestly, "you both know that you hold within you the Power to use these things."

"What was that word you told to us?"

"It is an old word for light. If you say it, willing light to come for you, then it will do so now."

"So, the way to use the Wards is to say old words, whilst making a wish." Said Chris. "Where do we learn more of these words?"

"Alas, I know only a few. If you point at someone and say RANGDOR then that person will freeze his or her movement, until released. HINGENDOR will release them, or any other who is trapped, provided your will and the Ward are stronger than whoever opposes you."

"OI," yelled an annoyed dwarf, slowly and very stiffly falling over.

"I didn't expect you to try it!" scolded Lakin, as Chris let his arm drop, looking shifty.

"Let me GO!" the dwarf yelled again, his vocal chords unaffected by the spell.

The Banned Underground gathered round the stricken dwarf with interest.

"He always was stiff necked."

"Stiff little finger too."

"Hey, I remember them!"

Linda kicked Chris hard on the ankle, and he muttered the word of release. The smitten dwarf relaxed, and then stood up glaring, and clearly upset about something. The Banned Underground moved a respectful distance back, away from the bad language.

"Can you remember those three words?" Lakin asked. "Others, as Linda has found, may rise unexpected from within the Ward itself in time of peril."

At last, they came to the Northern Wall. The Archway to the Passage held no Doors, but was richly carved. On the floor before the entrance to the passage lay a Golden Runesign, which flashed fire in the light from the wards of Lingard.

"What is that?" asked Chris, subdued.

"That is the Runesign Narselb, signifying the Circle of Life, both the beginning and the ending in symmetry everlasting."

"Like re incarnation?" asked Linda

"Who wants to come back as a plant?" scoffed Chris.

"Depends which plant," came an obvious comment from behind him.

Lakin turned away. "Linda, Chris, you have lit the cavern for some time now. Come, we will light the torches, and you may let the light go out."

"How do we do that?"

"Release your will from the Ward, and its power will fade."

Breaking their normal habits, the teenagers did as was suggested, and slowly as they passed the glowing Runesign and entered the Passageway, which led North, the light around them diminished.

"Cool," said Chris.

"Mine's hot," said Linda.

"Ouch! You're right!"

Before too long, the Passage twisted sharply to the right, and began to fall. Lakin held up his hand to halt the party, and then they began to go slowly down the slope, towards a glow reflected off the walls. Rounding a corner they entered a large well-lit cave to face a large group of heavily armed dwarfs all pointing spears at them.

"Halt!" came the order, and they all stopped.

"Why," grumbled Fungus, out of breath, "is no one ever pleased to see us?"

Chapter Nine

Unwilling to break a winning streak, the morning mist rolled in from the sea, obscuring the land and clouding the coastline in fogs. The locals were used to weather like this, and paid little attention, to the acute disappointment of the mist. Above the coast line the seagull (still there from the earlier chapter) had a cardiac arrest as a second gull appeared like a wraith out of the clouds.

"Jonathon Livingston, I presume?"

"Sqwark!" expired the first seagull, as the shock stopped its heart.

The cairn was silent as a stone, calciferous rock being less chatty by nature than the igneous variety. This explains why geologists are silent, withdrawn souls, with little small talk at parties. Shapes appeared dimly through the mist, and stopped near the cairn. The Tuatha were meeting.

"What are you doing here, Laeg?" asked Finn.

"Erald is still busy up in the Helvyndelve, so he made me leader for the day."

"Why you?"

"Probably because I'm the only one sober."

"Fair enough."

Laeg grunted as a time expired seagull landed upon his head. "Who threw that at me?"

Finn sneezed, loudly, and wiped his nose on his sleeve.

"Oh good grief. Do you have to do that? Why can't you carry tissues like anyone else?"

"No pockets in these robes, Liamm."

"Well, shove some up your sleeve."

"Not my fault. I nearly caught my death when we were here last."

"No, that was when you played darts with the Edern, and hit that Blear in the foot."

"'S Right. Look he gave you, could have nearly killed anyone."

"Won the game, though didn't we?"

"That wasn't the point."

"No, the point was the bit stuck in Blear's foot. Expensive shoes they were, too."

"All right." Laeg sounded unaccountably weary, and suddenly felt sympathy for Erald. "Anyone seen the Edern around?"

"No. We're all a bit early."

"If this weather gets worse, I'll be late."

"It's not fatal, you idiot."

"No, it won't kill me. I'll be late cos I'll be going home. I'd rather watch snooker on TV than hang around here."

The cairn took some offence at this, as would anything/anyone, and moved off to hide in the mist.

"Are you sure we are in the right place, Laeg? Can't see that blasted cairn anywhere now."

"It was here a moment ago, Diarmid. Ah, look, here they come."

Three of the Edernlords approached. "I say, Laeg, this mystic secrecy is all very well, but isn't there a decent restaurant we can meet at instead? And not get wet through every time? Do you know how hard it is to get rain marks out of these silken cloaks?"

"There's a chippy down the road," offered Finn.

Blear gave him a look. "Besides that awful pub, I expect." He sniffed.

"See? Blear caught the same cold as me."

"I rather doubt that. Yours will be a common cold, I expect, and I wouldn't have one of those."

"What sort of cold would you get then?"

"Investment bankers do not get colds."

"Why?" asked Finn.

"It's called non specific influenza in our office," said Hankey.

"So, not because you all own shares in Lemsip then?"

"This isn't making progress," said Laeg.

"The Bodgandor have not increased their strength," said Blear. "But there are very many of them."

"We feel that we should ride to the aid of the Dwarfs," said Laeg.

"Can't stand them myself," added Liamm, "but we cannot leave the Helvyndelve to fall to our enemies."

"I doubt that we have the strength to retake the Dwarf Halls if they fall to the Bodgandor," mused Blear.

"The last Auditor's report on our current availability was not encouraging," Meillar contributed.

"You are in essence correct," Hankey agreed. "In fact a period of retrenchment was suggested, before the final fiscal report, in case adverse comments were needed. Which would have a deleterious effect the value of the stocks. Should we enter a period of intense activity now, they might feel the need to issue a profits warning."

"The markets could turn against us."

"That could start a run."

Diarmid began to move away.

"Where are you going?" demanded Laeg.

"I'm starting a run, before I feel the need to issue a warning: in this case I'd thump one of them round the ear."

"Now there is no need to take that reaction. My colleagues are merely expressing their concerns over the holistic implications of any proposed action," chided Blear.

"But I haven't suggested anything yet."

"He couldn't get a word in sideways," muttered Liamm.

"How do you do that, then?"

"Dunno. Stand sideways, I suppose, and keep talking."

"Easy for you, then. You never shut up."

"At least I do contribute."

"Mainly complaints."

"I prefer to call it constructive criticism."

"Can we please get back to the point?" asked Laeg.

"If this lot are too afraid to help, there is no point in being here," said Liamm.

"How are insults going to help us?" asked Laeg

"Who says we are too afraid?" demanded Blear. "The Edern are *never* too afraid! Excessive timidity is as severe a corporate misdemeanour as excessive risk taking. There are times when it is important to take immediate radical restructuring within a market place, and prudent corporate governance requires a Chief Executive Officer to accept the responsibility for recognising the encroachment of commercial rivalry and antagonistic economic activity with a view to authorising urgent activity within the group to counter the perceived threat with effective remedial action, utilising the successful core abilities and adapting them (within a fluid environment if such a course appears to the senior management on the ground to be advisable) to ensure that the outcome reassures the stakeholders that the Board is able to make effective decisions without undue procrastination and adapt to a rapidly fluctuating market situation with advantage to maximise the ultimate returns for the corporation whilst protecting the core market share and continuing to maintain the strategy and mission statement set by the board with only minimal departures to react proactively to the threat posed by a nebulous but still potential hostile takeover."

There was a long silence. The other two Edernlords, who had been frowning at the earlier part of the statement, nodded in concerted agreement.

Finn turned to Liamm with a confused expression. "Two things bother me."

"What are they?"

"One: what the hell did all that mean, and two: how did he get it all out in one go?"

"Dunno what it meant, but I bet he's an Olympic prospect for holding your breath."

Laeg approached the subject with a little more tact. "Is there a condensed version?"

"Oh, you mean a Campbell?" replied Hankey.

"Sorry?"

"Is that a press release or a soup?" asked Diarmid.

"Whatever. The CEO replied quite concisely, I thought, outlining the basic provenance in the reasoning behind his decision to commit resources."

"He's at it now," complained Liamm. "Can't any of you bloody word merchants just speak in English?"

"It is scarcely the fault of the Edernlords if you Tuatha lack the skills required and necessary understanding of subtle matters within a boardroom environment, and hence regrettably experience a dearth of the appropriate language concomitant with such a position."

"I'm too thick to understand that, me," grumbled Finn

"I think that's what he said, actually," said Liamm, who was hanging on gamely to the conversation.

"Lord Blear," Laeg fought for understanding, "Is it then your intention to fight?"

"I just said that it was."

"See?" commented Liamm, to Finn. "It was constructive criticism. It made the pompous beggars fight!"

"We are here in the ancient heart of Sinadon, but even here we would be at war if Lord Telem did not hold the crossings," said Blear.

"I understood that," muttered Liamm, but was overheard.

"Then understand this, Tuatha. If it was not for the fighting power of the Edern, Bodgandor would be lose about your heels as you stand here today. This hallowed meeting place would be lost to you."

"I normally get lost trying to find it anyway, in this blasted mist."

"Shut up, Liamm. You are normally lost in the pub."

"Listen." Liamm finally lost his temper. "If you lot are going to fight with us, then better get your skates on. We know that Surdin's cub wizard has nicked the Amulet of Kings. If he gets to control it, then he'll have enough power to stamp us into the ground. His boss has enough Bodgandor hanging around trying to get through the Gate Between Worlds to crush your empire.

"Well we're not going to hang about. Erald has already been fighting a FireTroll in the Helvyndelve trying to get to the wizard, now it's your turn to help."

The Edern were quiet. Then Blear spoke: "I have said that we will fight. Lord Telem holds the crossings, so we will assemble our hosts, as we promised. Then we will fight our way across Sinadon towards the Helvyndelve and there make a stand with you. But if the Dwarfs lose their Halls before that, I am concerned that we may be adrift in the open with no refuge ahead or behind."

Laeg replied to him. "Lord Blear. The finding of the Amulet by Surdin has changed everything in our world. If they control its power, then they will visit on this world such a host of Bodgandor that we will never regain it from them."

"What of Rigor? What of the witches? Can they not help us?"

"Most of them are out of the country, along with most of Surdin's strength, and cannot be recalled in time."

"Then how does Surdin threaten us so, if they too are not here?"

"It seems to be a private deal done by the Grey Mage and his apprentice."

"Ah. Unregulated private enterprise. Strictly, quite acceptable outside of a planned economic environment."

"Consider them as rogue traders? Unlicensed operators?"

"Different matter. Can't have that. As I said, we have to take action. It will take two days until we are before the entrances to the Delve." Blear looked all around the area, wearing the expression that had given him his name. "This may be the last time I am in TalyBolion. The heart of our ancient kingdom. Mind you, it is a real dump and I cannot say how glad I for one would be to be rid of the place. The spot near Yr Wyddfa is much better. Don't suppose you'd make me an offer to take it out of our property portfolio?"

"No. What would we do with it?"

"You could redevelop."

"No thanks. Have you still got that power lead running into the Nuclear Reactor then?"

"Yes. Works a treat, and since they don't know we have the power take off, we don't get any bills. Well worth the occasional inconvenience."

"Such as?"

"Well, you know how carrots are supposed to help you see in the dark?"

"Yes."

"We can use ours as lanterns. And do NOT ask me about the funny shaped potatoes. The spouts were as big as tennis balls. And we had to stop growing parsnips."

"Let me guess. The shape?"

"No. The size. They kept coming up a foot long, and the girls made some *very* cutting remarks."

"Oh."

"Some of the boys keep talking about diversifying into alternative technology."

"Wind power?"

"No, we gave up on the sprouts too. The tide is flowing towards Wave energy now."

Finn waved his arm, and looked at it, bemused rather than energised. "Is that a Zen thing?"

Blear sighed. "Extracting energy from the waves in the sea is what I meant."

"Too risky. Everyone knows mixing water and electricity is dangerous."

"Of course it isn't."

"Then why do they keep putting up signs about it?"

"Here," put in Liamm, "My aunt, she was stood in some water when she accidentally got a shock. Nearly killed her."

"The electric shock?"

"Rather it was the shock of getting her feet clean, I think. Bit it was still dangerous."

"To whom?"

"Her, mostly. Just shows, you should never wash your feet with your boots on."

"I will try to remember that."

"See, you can learn something everyday! Even at our age."

"How old are you, Liamm?"

"Dunno, really. But I know that I am old enough to get served down the pub. See you lot later."

"Liamm," said Laeg, "we are about to leave to face dangerous and wicked enemies, and fight them to the death to try secure a future."

"Best have a strong double first then."

"And some crisps, on the side."

"Prefer nuts, really."

"You would, what with being nuts."

"That was predictable. You are getting old."

"But not as old as you are, so you can get the drinks in, in case the landlord twigs I am under age."

"Finn, you are over two thousand years old!"

"But I don't look it Liamm. Anyway, last time we were here, you didn't get a round."

"That's what you think."

"You never bought me one."

"No, I was too busy getting around the barmaid."

"Lucky git. Have to be a bit careful there, she's the landlord's daughter."

"Then after I've pulled her, maybe she'll pull us a few pints."

"Now *that's* what I call positive thinking."

"Finn, have you noticed something?"

"What?"

"They've all gone off and left us."

"Not very civil. Come on, let's get down the pub quick then, before they hog the bar." The two Tuatha headed away down the slopes. Erald watched them go, shaking his head. Then, alone in the mist, he joined the throng of Edern as the muster continued.

Hogging the bar was not, however, very high on the agenda for the Edern. A wine bar might have been different, of course, but no such refinement existed in the locality. A serious omission, and one that was high on the agenda. Blear had been busy giving orders, and soon the area close to the cairn began to fill up with Edern, their horses, and, well, what horses do second best.* So many horses gathered, in fact, that the well trampled fields became very, very fertile next year and the cairn so overgrown that it no longer felt the need to hide: instead it was more concerned with finding a way out.

[* First best is using up enormous sums of money.]

Also interested in finding the way out was Blear.

"What with this mist, and all these chaps milling about, I'm not sure of the way," Blear complained.

"I've got a GPS on my phone. That way's South," advised Hankey.

"I've never really trusted this modern technology. What's wrong with an old fashioned spell?" asked Meillar.

"Well, these are supposed to work anywhere, and tell you where to go."

"You mean it swears at you when you use it?"

"No. To be honest, it's more the other way round. It works better if *you* swear at *it.*"

"I knew a witch like that, once," said Meillar.

"Maybe it works by remote witch power. That would explain it. Anyway, that way is South."

"Any way suits me, as long as we can get out of this mist."

Lord Blear rose up in his stirrups, and in a mighty voice, called to his troops. "OK, Chaps! Follow me!"

"Just like being at school," observed Meillar.

"How so?" asked Hankey.

"Playing follow my leader with Blear. He always insisted on being in charge then. And usually got lost, too."

Blear waved his arm high, and trotted imperiously off into the mist. No one else moved. After a short pause, he trotted back into view. "Why didn't you tell me the cliff was that way?"

"We sort of thought you'd find out. South is over there."

With a scowl, the CEO set off again. This time, the mounted horde followed him, leaving the meadows lonely. With an effort, the cairn sneaked back to its original position, and sighed in relief. Then it received the blessings dropped by the overexcited seagull from overhead, a metaphor for all endeavour. Slowly at first, but as the mist fell away and all could see, somewhat faster, the Horde of the Edern rode towards the fords at Dinas Orwch. Meillar was tapping away on his Blackberry.

"What are you doing?" Hankey asked him.

"Just sending Telem a text to let him know we are on the way. But the signal's a bit iffy here, and the screen's a bit fuzzy too."

"Is that a Blackberry?"

"Yes."

"Should have got a Lemon. They're sharper."

"The acid test is if they work properly."

"Do you think we are going to win, Meillar?"

"To be honest, I don't know. Has that phone of yours got a future prediction app on it?"

"Well, it has, but I think it doesn't work too well. The Lottery numbers it gives me never come up, I know that. But on the other hand, it is very good at telling me when I'm getting lost."

"When's that?"

"All the time, really. And mostly thanks to the SatNav on it."

"Self fulfilling prophecy then. It tells you you're going to get lost, and then makes sure that you do. Maybe it's got something to do with the warranty."

"I tried complaining to the shop, and they hit me with the Terms and Conditions."

"And?"

"It hurt so much that I decided to stop complaining."

"Right. But to answer you, I don't know."

"I'm lost."

"What, already? No wonder you need a SatNav. No, I don't know if we are going to win. But I suppose it has to be better than doing nothing. So, we'll fight. And hope to win. First step is to join Telem at the Fords, and go on from there."

"Do you know what the SatNav co ordinates are?"

"Just leave it alone, and follow everyone else."

The horde rode on.

The scene moves on, shifting a little in focus now, to show a broad but very shallow stretch of water. Imagine the English Channel, but not as wide, and a boating lake, but not as deep. Perhaps not worth imagining that, then. Try a really big kitchen floor, after an industrial sized washing machine has sprung a leak. On either side of the water, trees rise on the banks with a narrow strip of what (for the want of a better word) we shall call sand between them and the water. On the strip of not quite sand, a line of the Edern stands at bay. Splashing towards them across the straits, like a group of demented redcoats on vacation from the holiday camp and determined to get revenge, come a lot of Bodgandor. On the far side, managing not to get his feet wet, stands the Grey Mage of Surdin. Why? Is there a deep meaning, or mere narrative convenience? In fact, he too was annoyed at not making the Mediterranean Convention this year, and was determined to work through his anger by wreaking vengeance on the North Wales Holiday Towns to which he had been condemned as a child. This would just have been the start, but he was frustrated by the inability of his remaining Bodgandor to cross the straits.

"Look" he snarled at them, "I could have left you to fight underground in the Lakes. Instead I brought you here, where the weather's better and there are shorter queues for the toilets. Now be fair, slaughter that lot, and we can all have a nice sit down and a pint."

Enthusiastically (for they had not yet tasted the local beer) the Bodgandor had attacked. But time and again, the Edern threw them back into the water. Now they kept going because they were convinced that there must be something on the other side of the tree line worth fighting for. If they had made it through the trees, and seen what lay before them, it might have been a different story. But they hadn't, so it wasn't. And the author has been saved from the excessive use of the "back" button on his keyboard, another bonus.

Shouting their WarCry (designed in every universe to raise the terror of a visit by the Jehovah's Witnesses)* the Bodgandor again stormed into the dwindling band of the Edern, who fought back ferociously.

[WarCry is actually published by the Salvation Army, but it's no use letting facts get in the way of a joke. The Jehovah's Witnesses publish Watchtower, not to be confused with (All along the) Watchtower, the classic Jimi Hendrix track. The content is different, although I suppose it might be possible for a schizophrenic to read one whilst listening to the other. I would not recommend it myself.]

Again, to the disappointment of the Grey Mage, the Bodgandor were thrown back into the water, and retreated. Lord Telem looked around his weary force with pride. "All we need to do," he addressed them, "is to stand firm and follow the mission statement. They will realise that their strategy is in vain."

His troops, in the manner of foot soldiers everywhere, were too busy to listen.

"Listen!" he shouted.

"What to?" asked one.

"Oh come along, you can't hope for promotion with grammar like that," his neighbour advised.

"I an so sorry, forgot myself for a moment. Must be because of this spear that is stuck in my arm."

"Well, it's harmless compared to poor syntax. That can be really damaging."

"I'll bear it in mind."

"Always glad to help."

"Good! Then grab hold of that end and pull. No, the end of the spear, you idiot." *

[* Warning. Grasping the sharp end of a spear may cause injury. A public service announcement Always complete a written three page risk assessment first. In triplicate.]

"I know what's wrong with you. Cough for me. Now, cough again. And again. Got it! You have a bad cough."

"Not just a spear in my arm, then?"

Through the trees came the sound of horses, and of course, arguments. The Host had arrived. Slowly, they filtered through the trees, complaining as the branches collided with their heads, and wondering whom the luckless landowner might be. One or two, who were solicitors when not fighting in mystical wars, wondered about making negligence or damage claims. However, on reaching the sand, they were quite content to stop still, and hurl abuse at the retreating Bodgandor.

On the far side of the water, the Grey Mage was incensed. His cherished dream of razing first Rhyl, then Bangor and lastly Abersoch to the ground with fire, sword, and his host of evil Bodgandor, and erasing the memories of his deprived childhood, was shattered. He hopped on the spot, cursed, and swore in disappointment. The bad language drifted across the straits to the Edern, who disapproved.

"I say, that's a bit strong," commented Blear.

"That too."

"And that never happened to *me* in Abersoch. Even though I tried," joined in Hankey.

Blear looked around the beach, at the bodies, bits of bodies, and unidentifiable things washed up by the sea, probably from Liverpool. "Not very scenic here, is it? Your chaps up to going on, Telem?"

"Of course."

"Then we'll find them some spare horses. Now that you have seen this lot off, we are going to go and sort out the Bodgandor that are trying to take over the Helvyndelve."

"Why?"

"Not sure that I fully appreciated every nuance of the reason," replied Hankey, ignoring the mildly rebellious comments behind him.

"Probably because he didn't listen."

"He never listened at school."

"Certainly doesn't in the Board Meetings."

"But," Blear raised his voice over the mutterings," the Tuatha have assured me it is the best thing to do."

"So that's all right, then."

"I have made the decision. There is no room for dissent."

"Do you know what a decision is, Meillar?"

"Go on."

"That's when you get fed up of thinking."

"Um. And dissent?"

"When you are fed up of the decisions."

"You know, Blear is a living proof that light is faster than sound."

"Why?"

"I thought he looked clever until I heard him speak."

"Hankey," ordered Blear, "take some of the chaps and see off the rest of that lot across the water."

"If you insist."

"I do."

Lord Hankey beckoned to a group of the mounted Edern, and splashed off in pursuit of the fleeing Bodgandor. The Bodgandor halted their flight, and again turned to face their foes. But then a horn sounded from the tree line behind the watching Edern, and a lone black clad horseman rode down across the sand, and into the water. He drew a great rune encrusted sword that flashed golden light across the sky as he swirled it around his head, and cantered towards the now still Edern and Bodgandor.

The lone horseman spurred his horse into a gallop, and sped past the fighting towards the far shore. But his opponent did not wait to receive him. Instead the Grey Mage bowed, crossed his arms across his chest, and vanished into the trees. The remaining Bodgandor scattered, and fled to follow him.

Hankey, his spear dripping red, rode to meet the black robed horseman. "Laeg, our thanks." He panted with the exertion – of the fight that is, not from having to thank Laeg.

"Glad I could help," replied Laeg, sheathing his sword. "The Grey Mage did not want to fight me. Twice now he has faced one of us and lost, and he failed also to gain the power of the ancient Wards in the safe keeping of the witch Grizelda. But were he to obtain those, or worse still, the Amulet of Kings, then he would have enough Power to overcome all of us Tuatha at once if his need arose."

"Then we must see that it does not."

"Lord Hankey, I look to you to ensure that Blear does not fail the bargain. The Tuatha are seeking the Amulet, to protect it from Surdin's clutches, and we need the aid of the Edern as never before. Do not let him fail."

Laeg turned, and before the other Edernlords, who were now riding across the straits towards them could draw close, he turned and, riding into the trees, also vanished from view.

"Where's he gone, then!" demanded Blear, pulling his horse up beside Hankey.

"Hunting." Hankey stared at the now empty trees in front of him. "Hunting."

"But he's not dressed properly! He's wearing black!"

Chapter Ten

In the kitchen, the kettle began to whistle cheerfully, in blatant defiance of its environment. Grizelda glared at the fridge, daring it to move whilst her back was turned, and then started to make herself a cup of tea. She was in the grip of a powerful, and unexpected emotion: she actually felt a little lonely, and concerned for others.

Witches are very good at empathy, but normally this skill is used to help terrify those who deserve it most; plumbers and those builders who suck air through their teeth in the now famous reverse whistle were her favourite targets. Taxi drivers came a close second, and anyone who worked for the Council also made the list. Their inmost fears revealed themselves easily to Grizelda, who could then magnify the fears into total all out naked terror, and help her get her own way. Rarely did she have to queue in the shops, the other customers would quietly – or if they had experienced her before, noisily – drop their shopping, desert their trolleys and abandon wallets and purses to get away. Picking up such unconsidered trifles helped her budget, though not her waistline.

But Grizelda was worried tonight. The teenagers were away, lost in the depths of the Helvyndelve with a jazz loving BogTroll and some suspect dwarfs. Or at least the kind of dwarf most likely to be a suspect. Her husband, who could often be late home from the pub if he bumped into a friend, acquaintance, someone he once met twenty years ago for ten minutes, or anybody at all really, was also adrift in the dwarf mines: In this case in the company of an alcoholic Irish Fairy, who enjoyed a good fight. Or a bad fight, come to that. Any old fight at a pinch.

This was not reassuring either.

The kettle whistled again, so she glared at it until, abashed, the kettle moved from the hot hob, which turned itself off. Grizelda picked up the pot of tea, and walked back into the living room. Placing the pot carefully on the table, she wandered over to the window, and stared out over the lake, watching the sun's last rays turn the water golden. She poured the tea, and returned to watch the sunset. The lake was still and placid, unlike her thoughts.

As she turned away to pour the tea a flash of movement caught her eye. Two horsemen were riding hard up the valley, staying close to the trees. She watched carefully for some time, then relaxed slightly as she recognised two of the Tuatha. But then she gasped, spraying tea all over the wall and one of the occasional chairs, now in receipt of an unexpected cleaning. One horse had reared up, throwing the rider. But the second stopped, turned back for a moment, and then continued on towards her, now with the first rider behind him.

Close to the cottage, some dark shapes swarmed up out of the heather, but the pillion rider swung his sword (almost removing his colleague's right ear in the process) and the dark shapes fell back. The Tuatha rode onwards away from the press, but arrows fell about them as they passed into the dubious safety of the garden.

"Open!" commanded Grizelda forcefully, and the door flew back, bounced off the wall, and neatly smacked into the face of Lugh Longhand.

"Shot!" exclaimed Malan, his brother.

"Just lucky," replied Grizelda, modestly.

"No, you daft witch, I mean he's been shot."

"Got a broken nodes now, too," complained Lugh, holding his left arm with his right hand, and streaming blood down his face. He could have got a job as an extra in any TV soap looking for accident victims.

"Accidents happen. Let's have a look at that arm. No, just a flesh wound. We'll bind it up with some of my special paste, and you will soon be right as a trivet."

Lugh looked alarmed. "Is that the paste that turns people into frogs?"

"I said trivet, not rivet."

"Don't want to be an iron table stand, either."

"I won't stand for this rubbish. Pull your sleeve up, sit down, and drink some tea."

Lugh and Malan stared suspiciously at the teapot. Which glared back at them. Grizelda snorted, and the teapot shrugged, and poured two more cups of tea. The Tuatha both added a lot of sugar before drinking, whilst Grizelda (expertly, it must be said) bandaged the wound. Outside, the cheated Bodgandor practised their woodcraft skill by trying to barbeque the horse. The skills being nearly as rusty as the BBQ, the horse got away instead.

"You've done this before," Malan observed, watching the first aid.

"Ben will insist on doing DIY. I keep telling him that it's easier if I just hex whatever it is he's trying to do, but he won't have it. Even when his shelves fall off the wall. On top of him, sometimes. Honestly, there are times I have to hex things back together when he's not looking. And Fungus, he's as bad."

"Fungus?"

"You know, the BogTroll who plays saxophone."
"Oh, him. You remember him, Lugh. Came round to our place once, got Finn so drunk he couldn't walk straight for a week."

"Yeah, got him now. Plays good sax though. His take on Green Onions is worth a hear."

"Not when the vegetable patch tries to come in to listen," said Grizelda, decisively. "An' when he's here he keeps fiddling around with that old motorbike in the woodshed. The times I've had to have a go at him over the oil stains."

"Oil stains? So it's not a Japanese then?" asked Lugh, interested.

"No. I told you, it's a motorbike."

"I meant a Japanese motorbike."

"If it belongs to that Fungus, it's probably just a funky moped," put in Malan.

"Oh, I dunno. But I know he behaves as if it were precious, instead of a piece of oily junk. And he won't let me fix it with magic, either."

"I'll have a look in a moment, out of interest," said Lugh.

"As long as you are careful with it. Or I'll never hear the last of it."

Grizelda tied off the bandage with a professional flourish, and sat down again on a chair (which groaned. First second hand tea, and now this). "So, what news from the Helvyndelve? Me husband and me nephew an' niece are in there."

"Well, we know about your husband. He and Erald fought a FireTroll to a draw, and now he's trying to put together a counter attack."

"Won't work. He's always been useless behind a counter. Just ask them at Tesco, The kids?"

"We spoke only briefly with Erald. We know only that they were with the BogTroll and Lakin before the attack."

"If they are with Lakin," put in Malan, seeing the look on the witch's face, "they will be as safe as anyone within the Helvyndelve."

"That's not much comfort. Anyway, why are you here?"

"Erald sent us to help protect you."

"And why does he feel I need it? Be warned, if either of you evens *thinks* the phrase 'a woman on her own', you'll be sat in a pond looking for flies and going 'Rivet Rivet' before you know it."

"Erald knew that you held two magical Wards in safekeeping. The Grey Mage…"

"What, him?" interrupted Grizelda. "I've been havin trouble with his juniors and trainees all summer. None of them made it very far. Although that Ned once got into the Kitchen. Brave lad. He didn't stop though, which was a shame."

"Why?"

"I was running short of a few things, and he could 'ave been the basic ingredients."

Malan swallowed hard. "The Grey Mage" he continued, "knows you hold the Wards. Twice now he has faced Erald, and twice lost. Erald fears that he will seek out some device to gain Power, and the wards you protect would do nicely for him. Perhaps the trouble you have had was his way of probing your defences."

Grizelda laughed. "Then he really didn't try too hard. I mean, some of his lads were trying to read the spells out of a book!"

"Not all Surdin's followers and allies are so weak."

"No, that Ned did get hold of a Taxman. Soon got rid of him, though."

"How did you do that?" asked Malan, impressed.

"My chapter head is proof reading his boss' next book. So I gave him a call."

"Your White Witch leader is proof reading an evil wizards' manual?"

"Yep. Didn't say he were correcting the errors, did I?"

"Anyway," continued Malan, "Erald thought that to send you some aid now would be of benefit to us all."

"If he wanted the Wards of Lingard, then he's too late."

"Have they been taken?" Lugh looked worried.

"Yeah. Fungus gave them to the kids."

"Was that wise or safe?"

"Who knows? But it has happened now, so there's not much we can do about it, until we get the kids back. And they are lost in the Helvyndelve, you say."

"We didn't actually say that they were lost…"

"But you don't know where they are, do you?"

"Well, not as such."

"Lost covers it, then. We'll just have to wait until they are found."

"Unfortunately, something else that was lost has been found."

"Normally, I just buys a replacement."

"The Amulet of Kings."

"What, that old thing? That's been gone for years."

"But now Ned has found it, and vanished."

"I didn't know it could do that."

"No, I meant that he has fled without giving the precious thing to his boss, The Grey Mage."

"So he's in for it, if he's found. Why are you not all out there looking for him?"

"Most of us are. But Erald thought that some of us should guard the places he might go to, and this is one of them. Well protected, isolated, and therefore secure and private."

"Ah, I get you. The Amulet does internet porn."

"No of course not. He needs somewhere to attune to its powers. This place would be ideal, were you not here. Hence we two have come to help you."

"I see. Well, I suppose you'd better make yourselves comfy. I'm gonna see to the goat. Just take care if you go into the Kitchen."

"Why, what's in there?"

"Ben's homebrew. And it's feeling explosive, so don't go near the bottles."

Grizelda got to her feet (a sigh of relief came from the chair, but the Tuatha misinterpreted the noise and looked embarrassed) and stomped out of the room, calling to the goat.

"Well, that went better than we thought," Lugh said.

"Yes. Probably your wound helped."

"We told her that we had been sent to help protect her, and neither of us has a tongue a foot long. Result, in my book. Is there any more of that tea?"

"Yes," replied the teapot.

"Well, pour me some please. I feel like I need a pick-me-up."

His chair wobbled slightly, then rose two feet into the air.

"That's not what I meant!"

Malan looked around hastily, and then spotted a small bottle of Glenfiddich whisky, half full, on a side table. As the chair landed, with all the elegance of a trainee pilot putting a jumbo jet full of passengers onto a wet runway at nighttime, Malan poured the contents of the bottle into Lugh's cup, admiring the colour. Lugh drained it in one gulp, and his colour slowly returned to normal. Grizelda, alerted by the noise, came back into the room.

"Honestly, you two are not fit to be left for two minutes. And what have you done with this bottle?"

"Well, Grizelda, Lugh wasn't feeling too well, so I added some whisky to his tea."

"Not from that bottle you didn't. That was my sample for the doctor."

Lugh's face set, and then he jumped up, and out of the open window. He could then be heard being noisily sick onto the flowerbed. The rambling rose struck back, and his face was covered in scratches when he came back into the room. Malan poured more tea, with a contented look.

Grizelda opened a cupboard, and removed a fresh bottle. Lugh leant back in his chair, but the bottle was new and sealed. Or at least, for as long as any sealed bottle of malt whisky stays sealed in the presence of two of the Tuatha, which is to say, not very long. Slowly, the tension drained out of the atmosphere in the room, and all three began to relax. Too soon, of course. Three heavy blows fell on the front door.

"Open, to the Power of Surdin," demanded a voice.

"Is that one of them maths things, you know, like 3 to the power of 5? Never understood them, myself." Malan's education was showing.

Lugh looked out of the window, before shutting it, hastily. "The garden is full of Bodgandor!" he exclaimed.

"Blast. They'll wreck the lawn."

Malan and Lugh looked at each other. The grass was so high that the lawn could have been profitably rented out to the SAS as a jungle environment for training.

"I ask again, Unlock the door."

"Persistent beggar. Wonder who he is?"

"Bet he plays the bass guitar for them."

"Why do you say that?"

"He can't find the key."

"This is the Third, and the last offer. Open the Door to us, and we may spare your lives."

"Get lost," called back Lugh, as he and Malan grabbed their weapons. Grizelda shook her arms free in her sleeves, and put on her black hat.

"What is your name?" called Grizelda, through the letterbox.

"My name is immaterial."

Grizelda looked at Lugh and Moran. Both shook their heads. "Never heard of you."

All three heard the roar of rage though. The door burst open, to reveal a FireTroll blazing with anger, in the porch. Grizelda raised her arms, and moments later; a heavy rain began to fall. The FireTroll snarled, but retreated to the shelter of the stone shed at the end of the garden.

"Knew there was a reason it always rains round here," said Lugh.

Then he became a little preoccupied, as Bodgandor stormed the kitchen door. Grizelda surrounded herself with a protective green power cone, and the first Bodgandor to enter the kitchen bounced off her, and had an unfortunate experience with the fridge. The second cannoned off the cone, lost its footing, and with a despairing wail, fell slowly into the cauldron of curry, never to be seen again.

As the Tuatha practised their swordplay, Grizelda grabbed the crate of homebrew and started lobbing bottles into the darkness. Unsure if these were halftime refreshments or weapons, the Bodgandor stopped to examine the bottles: which started to explode as the gasses in the liquid tormented by the action of being thrown across a garden, expressed their feelings. One of the Bodgandor managed to drink the contents of a bottle,* but then wished he hadn't. Others, showered by glass and bottle tops and covered in a strange smelling froth, turned and ran.

[* we are unable to call the stuff beer, as its resemblance to a refreshing, delicate liquid for drinking on social occasions was non existent]

"Biological warfare!" one complained.

"I thought that was Outlawed."

"Good Film that."

"What, Outlawed?"

"No, the one about biological warfare."

"Thought that was Germ Warfare."

"From Germ any?"

"Not really, no."

"Honest, I'm not drunk on duty," burbled he who had tasted the brew.

"Poisoned, possibly."

"Look out, she's got another crate of the muck."

The Bodgandor withdrew further. Grizelda slammed the kitchen door shut, and darkness fell on the garden.

"Isn't this far enough yet?" The FireTroll was becoming fed up of wandering around the Helvyndelve, with only Ned and a few Bodgandor for company.

"I think the way out is around the next bend."

The FireTroll threw a handful of flames ahead, down the very long and very straight tunnel ahead of them. "The next bend."

"That's what the map said. But it isn't drawn to scale."

"Look at this sorry lot. They'll never make it."

"Oh well."

Ned marched them along for a while, and then the tunnel did indeed bend. Just a little, but enough for the FireTroll to start arguing again. Ned silenced him by pointing to an archway, a hundred yards away on their right. But when they got there, the archway was full of carven, well dressed stone (or at least better dressed than Ned – the FireTroll didn't even make the shop door).

"Why do they have to hide *everything*?" grumbled the FireTroll.

"Open sesame!" commanded Ned. The arch of stone was unmoved.

"Oh come on. That one never works," sneered the FireTroll.

"Pretty bauble," coaxed Ned, holding up the Amulet, then trying again. "Dissocio!" "Agapia." "Agor."

The FireTroll sniggered, loudly.

"Hang on, I must know a few more."

"Try thinking like a dwarf."

"How do you think small? Crouch?"

"Nah, he's a tall footie player. Wrong approach. Think stupid."

"Dunno if I can do that."

"I'd have thought it came naturally."

Ned picked up the Amulet, and held it close to his face, peering at it. He leant against the walled up arch for balance, and fell straight through as the wall shimmered and vanished. With a cry, the FireTroll leapt through before the wall regained its substance, narrowly avoiding squashing Ned further into the peat bog on which he sprawled. "Seems like I've bin here before," grumbled Ned then got to his feet with a smug look on his face. "I did it! Oh yeah, I did it!" he started to jump for joy, then stopped in mid leap as he realised his feet were rising – but his wellies remained firm in the ground. His right foot resumed contact as instructed, but the left flailed around, and then with a sickening squelch plunged up to the knee in the peat. The sniggering FireTroll, who had quickly and efficiently made it to drier ground, and now sat on top of a pile of rocks enjoying the view, only increased his displeasure. Grasping the abandoned Wellington boot, Ned made his way out of the bog.

"Let's move along a bit, there's a dreadful pong here," said the FireTroll. "Oh, hang about, it's you."

"All right, that's enough. Where are the Doors? I'd like to know how to get back inside."

They both looked around. Of the Doors of the Dwarfs, there was no sign. The grassy fell rose, dark and bleak, towards Clough Head. A low pile of rocks lay in a jumbled heap, and in the middle distance a few lost sheep grazed peacefully.

"Good question, that," said the FireTroll, slowly.

"Well, we both fell into the bog here." Ned pointed at the slowly filling holes that marked his welly free passage. "So, that pile of rocks must be where the Doors are." Both walked slowly around the pile, but could see no sign that the Doors had ever been there.

"If we came out, we can get back in." The FireTroll jumped headlong at the rockpile, only to bounce off.

"Keep on knocking but you can't come in," said Ned, in revenge for the earlier insults.

"We might have to come back another day and try again," admitted the now bruised FireTroll.

Ned pulled a rather crumpled, and now slightly dog-eared map out of a pocket, and squeezed some water out of it. He then spread it out on a stone, and examined it carefully. "WE seem to be here, and the Circle at Dinas Tewet is THERE, so let's go that way."

They crossed a small beck, and trudged along a track. The FireTroll was thinking, always a bad sign in a flaming rock. "Look," he said, pointing to the looming bulk of Skiddaw to their left.

"It's a fell. They're all over the place. You can't move without falling over a fell here."

"Can tell you've fell over one. And that's the point. We are a bit conspicuous here. Let's go and hide up in that old Barn until night comes."

"You could be right. And I could do with a rest."

Ned and the FireTroll entered the old bothy, and found somewhere to lie down. Ned pulled out the Amulet of Kings, and studied it hard, trying to worm his mind into the precious thing. The FireTroll amused himself by staring at the pile of bracken on which Ned lay, until it burst into flames.

"Will you cut that out!" Ned exclaimed, after beating the flames out of his cloak for the fourth time.

"Sorry. Just seems to happen."

There was a silence for some time, for which Ned was grateful.

"Why does your boss want that Trinket, anyway?"

"What you call a trinket is possibly the most powerful magical artefact in this world."

"What did the dwarfs use it for, then?"

"Mainly to take the trash out, I think."

"I can see that. Having been through those Halls of theirs, there's a hell of a lot of trash to be cleared."

"Yeah. You could make a fortune, just delivering pizza to them."

"It's not a bad idea, if this Amulet thing doesn't work out. Being a FireTroll, it would be no problem keeping the food hot. The cheese goes all manky when it gets cold."

"Is it dark enough outside for us to get on yet?"

"Give it a go." The FireTroll seemed distracted by the thought of making a lot of ready cash.

"Look, if I can get control of this thing, we can make ourselves richer than we ever dreamed."

"I'm pretty hot at dreaming."

"You would be, what with being a FireTroll."

The two left the gently steaming bothy, and headed off up the track. The sun was now sinking below the western fells, but neither had an inclination to stare at the beauty of the sunset. The FireTroll showed a major attribute now, being able to glow in the dark, without first sitting in the core of a thermo nuclear reactor for half an hour.

"You any good at baked potatoes?"

"Shut up."

"Just peckish, that's all."

By Tewet Tarn, the FireTroll halted. Ned went on alone, and peered down the slope towards his goal. He cursed.

"What's up?"

"The place is full of humans."

"You said you were peckish. Me too."

"You can't eat them. There's too many of them."

"I could take a doggy bag home?"

"No."

"Please?"

"Still no. There's a chance some might get away, and raise the alarm. I need a couple of hours peace and quiet with the Amulet, not having to waste a couple of hours explaining you to the Police."

"I could eat them, too."

"No. The helmets would stick in your teeth."

"Spoilsport."

"Look, see that hillside there? The Grey Mage is planning to bring as many Bodgandor as he can get through the Gate to that spot, for a last attack on the Helvyndelve. The whole hillside will be crawling with eyes, by now."

"How do eyes crawl? I thought they just sort of rolled about. And they sort of squish if you stand on them."

"How many eyes have you ever stood on? No, on second thoughts, I don't want to know."

"Back at Trollheim, we use them on the snooker table sometimes, if we can't find the right balls."

"Which ones are the right ones? No, don't tell me, I don't want to know."

"Suit yourself. Are those humans still there, then?"

"Nah, they're goin back to the coach now. Bet they're off to the pub next."

"Lucky them."

"Come on."

Ned and the glowing FireTroll made their way cautiously towards the stone circle, and vaulted over the low wall that surrounded the stones. The last rays of the setting sun shone coldly red on the ancient stones.

"One of the Old One's places this," said the FireTroll, looking round. "It's a bit spooky."

"You're a FireTroll. Whatever can you find spooky?"

"Oh, you know. Just stuff."

"Stuff?"

"You don't want to know."

"Yes I do."

The FireTroll bent and whispered in Ned's ear. His face went a bit green.

"I didn't want to know that."

"Told you so."

"Go into the trees, and get a couple of branches for me. Not too big, mind."

The FireTroll wandered off, into the line of trees, and collected some small branches, then went back to the circle.

"Did you hear a noise, just then?" asked Ned, suspiciously.

"No."

Ned fumbled in a spare pocket, and brought out several sticks of Rowan. A further pocket revealed a quantity of ash wood, and a last pocket disgorged some bright yellow barbeque briquettes. (Marked on the packet ' for the wizard in a hurry'). A cigarette lighter came from the robes as well, and a few cones of sandalwood incense.

"Where did you get that from, the SAS?" asked the FireTroll. "Do you always carry all that lot around in those robes?"

"Just a habit I got into."

Ned carefully arranged the collection into a ritual fire on top of the fallen altar stone.

The FireTroll sneezed. "Sorry. Must have been that bog we fell in."

Ned carefully rearranged the collection into a ritual fire on top of the fallen altar stone.

"I said sorry. It's the damp. Doesn't agree with me."

Ned clicked at the lighter, several times, then swore loudly and threw it as hard as he could towards the trees. "Thought I heard a noise again," he said, still suspicious. Dirty deeds may be done dirt cheap, but they do foster sneaking suspicions. "I knew you'd come in useful," he grumbled to the FireTroll. "Light that. Carefully."

The FireTroll poked the construction with a finger, and slowly smoke started to arise, as the briquettes began to smoulder, with a vivid yellow/gold glow.

"Now we're cooking!" exclaimed Ned.

"Good. I'm still a bit peckish."

"We'll eat later."

The twigs now crackled with the rising flames, and Ned removed from yet another pocket a small jar of powder. There was a label on the jar, but the writing was small and curly, and difficult to see. It seemed to go all around the jar, several times.

"How can you read that?" asked the FireTroll.

"It's not hard. It's Copperplate writing."

"The coppers I know don't write like that. Especially on plates."

"How do you know any coppers?"

"The local nick took on some Goths in an affirmative minority recruitment policy drive. Saved a lot of money, cos they usually had their own uniforms and handcuffs already. Some of them come to the gigs we do as an Alice Cooper tribute band. Our bass player is the one you sent to have a go at the cottage by the lake."

"What do you play?"

"I'm the clever one. So I'm the manager. Means I get to count the money whilst they're all shouting abuse at each other."

Ned shook his head in despair, and very carefully pulled the stopper from the jar. "Don't ever let this stuff get on you," he warned the FireTroll. "Most of the label is just a Government Health Warning." He carefully emptied a small quantity of powder over the blaze. At once the flames leapt high into the air, and swirled around the stone circle, illuminating every standing (or fallen) stone with a yellowgreen aura.

"OMNENIVEROR," intoned Ned.

"MUNDENDIVEROR."

"MUNDENDELGROR."

He paused for breath, and the aura grew into an aurora that formed a flickering dome over the whole circle. Blackness grew beside the altar stone, in the shape of a mound formed by the absence of light.

"FUNCTATOR."

"IACET! IACET! IACET!"

The flames had gone, but each stone glowed as if from within with an unpleasant green light. The Dark Mound had almost a physical presence now, and Ned lowered his arms, and bowed before the entrance. He had no mystical need to do so, but it was a good effect, and hid his urgent need to clutch his chest pains.

*

Lakin walked over to where Chris and Linda lay asleep, and wondered about waking them up.

"You know what they say," advised Fungus, from just behind him. "Let sleeping teenagers lie."

"I thought it was dogs?"

"Teenagers are more likely to bite."

"What are we going to do with them, Fungus?"

"Don't suppose we could leave them here. Grizelda would never forgive me. An' as she's got me bike in her shed, that could prov awkward."

"Dunno what you want that thing for."

"Everyone needs to have a hobby."

"Everyone needs a job, too, but that's never affected you."

"I'm a professional musician."

"Case proved."

"What's your job then Lakin? All you've ever done is hang around being a bloody nuisance, except when you sing (badly) or when you sloped off for all that time."

"I'm the heir to the throne. That is doing my job."

"Give you that one."

"Look Fungus, you know where we're gonna have to go. And when we get there, there's probably gonna be more fighting. Is it right to take them?"

"Lakin, what are the chances of getting them back to the Witch's Cottage?"

"Zip."

"And if we leave them here with this lot, what happens if the Bodgandor come down that passage?"

"Nothing. It only leads to the bogs."

"Alright. *That* passage, then."

"OK, I take your point."

"And they do have those things round their necks. They seemed to be protected in that rumble in the Throne Room."

"You didn't seem to be a lot of help, Fungus."

"I had to look after the sax. Linda looked after you, or rather she sorted that Troll out for you."

"True. Got any of that Mint Cake left?"

"Your thugs emptied my pack."

"Fungus."

"Oh, all right." Fungus reached up, took off his baseball cap, extracted an emergency bar and broke it in half. He offered half to Lakin, who took it with only a small (dwarf sized) shudder of distaste.

"Tastes OK to me," said Fungus, eating his portion.

Lakin bit a piece off the end, and chewed thoughtfully. When something bizarre, unpleasant or downright nasty failed to happen to him, he ate the rest. Haemar, chewing something dwarfish, joined them.

"So, what's the score?" he asked.

"We're not having a gig now," replied Fungus.

"Obviously. There's nothing to drink except water. But what are we gonna do now? The lads we met here haven't had any trouble, but that can't last."

"We still have to fulfil our quest," said Lakin. The other two looked at him askance.

"You can't go round saying things like that," advised Fungus. "Next you'll be talking about destiny an' stuff."

"Fungus, as a child, I knew I had a Destiny."

"I was too poor," said Haemar.

"Destiny's Child? Not my cup of tea," said Fungus.

"Dunno, I quite liked the one on the left."

"We must pursue the evil sorcerer and recover the Amulet of

Kings," insisted Lakin.

"You know, Haemar, I just knew he was going to say that."

"Saw it coming, myself. Couldn't duck in time."

"So, are you with me then?" asked Lakin, still with a strange fire in his eyes, that Fungus put down to the effect of the Kendal Mint Cake.

"When's the next gig, Haemar, and have we been paid for it?" asked Fungus. "Oh, all right, I'm in. And we'll have to take these two, because it's too risky to leave them behind. Also, I'm too scared of Grizelda to let them out of my sight."

"Right then," said Lakin, decisively. "We'll take the dwarfs that came with us, and some of the ones we found here. The rest can stay to guard this exit." He walked over to the dwarf who was nominally in charge. "We are leaving on my quest. Lend me twenty of your lads. The Rest of you are to stay here to guard this Passage and the exit, in case any of a defeat in the Western Delve – others may need to retreat this way."

"Yes, Lord," replied the Commander. "Will you be returning this way? If so, we should set a password."

"If we are in a hurry, we'll have forgotten it. If not, it won't matter."

"Passwords are traditional."

"How about: Open the Door, Moron?"

"Anyone could try that. And how did you know my name?"

"Lucky guess."

Fungus rooted through his pockets, desperate for inspiration. Finding a bit of plastic, he read the wording. "American Express."

"That'll do nicely," said the Commander.

"How did you get an Amex Card?" asked Haemar.

"Found it near the lake. It's great for the adjusting the carburettor on the motorbike, that's all I use it for."

"Time to go." Lakin gently woke Linda, and less gently woke Chris.

"What's to eat?" asked Linda.

"Bread and cheese."

"Don't like cheese."

"Well, in a couple of hours, I'll take you to MacDonalds."

"OK," Linda replied, calming down a little. "I'll eat the bread and cheese anyway, if that's OK?"

Lakin doled out the food around everyone, to a muted chorus of grumbles and complaints. "Look, would you rather we went on a dangerous but vital quest to recover the Talismanic and Powerful Amulet of Kings, or to Pizza Express?"

There was a certain amount of low-level discussion just below hearing. "Mine's a pepperoni."

"Depends if it's deep pan. Can't abide deep pan."

"What about the chippy instead?"

"Look," bargained Lakin, "when I get the Amulet back, and I am King under the Mountain, I'll get a Pizza Hut franchise in. How about that?"

This was greeted more enthusiastically.

"And MacDonald's, then, though I'll probably need a bank loan to get both."

Now he sensed he had carried the audience with him. The lone dwarf raising the subject of a vegetarian option lost the argument when a hammer bounced off his (unhelmeted) head. Lakin gathered his party together, and now with a stronger warband than before, resumed his quest. They soon reached a low arch, similar to that which had impeded Ned earlier. Lakin knew the secret passcodes though, and quickly marched through the Doors out onto the open fells.

"Getting parky," observed Fungus.

"I didn't know BogTrolls felt the cold," said Felldyke.

"Course we do. We can be affected by anything that affects water. I froze once, having a fag outside a gig in Scotland."

"What happened?" asked Linda.

"Well, that was easy. Haemar poured whisky over me until I melted."

"What did you do then?" Felldyke wanted to know.

Fungus looked at Felldyke as if he was dense, then recalled he was a drummer. "Drank the whisky of course."

"Right."

Lakin led the small party across the fell under the darkening sky. Chris and Linda stayed beside Fungus, as his faint glow helped them avoid putting their feet into anything rural. They crossed a small stream, and Lakin led them east. At last, a line of trees appeared, with a low wall beside them. At an urgent signal from Lakin, they all dropped to the floor, and stayed very still. Dimly they made out a glowing figure emerge from the trees and have a good look around, then grab some branches and merge back into the trees.

"What was that?" asked Chris, quietly.

"FireTroll," answered Haemar.

Lakin pointed to one of his guards, who nodded, and slipped silently over the wall, and into the trees. After a few minutes, he returned. "The trees are only a thin screen," he hissed into Lakin's ear. "Then comes another wall, and then Dinas Tewet itself."

Lakin waved, and they all climbed over the wall.

"Can't you be quiet!" they all muttered at Felldyke.

"Not my fault. That stone fell over when I just looked at it."

They stole into the trees. Felldyke pushed forward, but stopped when a ballistic cigarette lighter clanged off his helmet. "And don't blame me for that, either!"

The sky lit up, as the magelight summoned by Ned flared around the circle.

"Wendfire!" exclaimed Fungus. "Lakin, you know what he's trying to do!"

"Let's hope he forgot the manual, and makes a mistake."

"That's no good. It's all automated these days. They just buy this kit; Grizelda showed me the catalogue once. Add water here, bit of Wendfire there, Bob's yer Uncle."

"You can change your DNA profile?"

"Yeah. Caer Surdin invented it to get their staff off drink driving charges."

"Bit anti social."

"Works though. Do you want a copy? It's mail order."

"Drat. Postmen won't deliver to us."

"You could use DHL."

"Hush!" Lakin bent forward, becoming even smaller, and hurried to the edge of the low wall surrounding the Stone Circle. The others joined him, and stared in astonishment at the eldritch, glowing stones and the dark Black Mound that lurked beside the Altar Stone. "Ned will have entered the Black Mound," said Lakin. "I must follow him. Linda, would you give me your Ward of Lingard, for I may need its power on that journey."

Linda was silent.

"Linda?"

"No. But I will come with you," she stared at the Black Mound. "If I didn't go in there, I wouldn't have a great story to make my mates jealous at school."

Fungus looked very gloomy. "That means me too."

"Aren't you scared?" asked Haemar, impressed.

"Bloody terrified, mate. But I'm more scared of what Grizelda would do to me if I didn't go with them."

"That's good thinking. I'd better come too."

"That's more than enough," said Lakin. He turned to the other dwarfs, and ordered them into positions around the wall, but told them on no account to enter the circle until the Stones lost their fire.

"We could be here a while," said Scar to Felldyke.

"Why?"

"That Keef Richards is old enough for a bus pass, and he's still on fire."

"Well, smoking, anyway."

Lakin led his chosen four into the Stone Circle. "Do not touch the Stones," he advised them.

"They're freezing!" said Linda as she passed close to one.

Lakin pointed at the Black Mound. "That does not really belong here. In fact, it isn't really here at all, but Ned summoned it and in a way part of it responded. It will remain until all who enter it here have returned to this world, or..."

"Or what?" asked Chris.

"Are no longer able to do so," said Lakin, grimly.

"Fine. Just so I understand what I'm getting into."

"That would need a couple of year's intensive study."

Chris shuddered. "Sounds like hard work."

"What is in there?" asked Linda.

"We will meet stairs leading downwards. Remember this, if we separate at all. The way out is always upwards, and steps, stairs, passages, anything that leads upward will in time take you out of the Mound. Inside, we will meet dangers, temptations and terrors to be overcome."

Linda threw back her blonde hair, aggressively.

"In time, we will come to a place at the bottom of the stairs where the wind blows, and the surf crashes endlessly upon the strand," continued Lakin.

"Life's a beach," muttered Fungus, still gloomy.

"Remember that most of the apparitions we will meet are merely illusions, and an iron will and steely resolve will win us past them."

Lakin stood at the entrance to the Dark Mound, and held up a lamp. They could all see a narrow stairway, leading downwards. Lakin drew a deep breath, and stepped forwards. The other four followed him.

Chapter Eleven

The dwarfs were getting restless. Several hours had gone past since the FireTroll had sealed the stairway to the Chamber of the Throne with a Runesign, and still it remained intact. The Bodgandor were now becoming a little more confident, and occasional arrows were fired up the stairs. Twice Erald had tried to break the Runesign, but each time had failed. Ben had also tried once, but had fared no better.

"If at first you don't succeed," said Ben.

"Hide the evidence?"

"We can't do that though, can we. Too many witnesses."

"So, we have to try again. And this time, get it right. Let's review what we did. I tried a water spell."

"I tried a darkness spell."

"I went for a basic counter enchantment."

"So, this time, a full-on counter blast?"

"It will take both of us."

Daran the Dwarf appeared at Erald's side. "There are whispers," he said quietly.

"Careless, I presume?" asked Ben.

"I couldn't care less," said Erald.

"Some of them are bothered that you have not yet broken the Runesign. They think that you might fail in the task. That you are not up to it any more."

Anger flared in Erald. "What!"

"Well, it is still there. Many of the lads here lost friends or brothers, sometimes both, in the fighting. They want revenge, and that is in their way."

"Tell them, then, to make ready," replied Erald. "Sharpen their weapons, for shortly we will lead the attack."

"That is well. But we have had scouts arrive here from the Darnil Vale Doors. There has been fighting in the Western Passage behind us, and a troop of cursed Bodgandor even made it as far as the First Great Western Cavern."

"Several were found slain, but it is not known for sure who killed them. A rumour has it that Lord Lakin passed that way, with several others, but reports are confused. What is certain is that two of Lord Lakin's bodyguard visited the guard post, and took stores, claiming them for Lakin."

"Now that is good news," exclaimed Ben.

"Excellent," agreed Erald. "Now we shall break this Runesign, for there is hope now that the Amulet will be found."

"But it has been found," objected Daran.

"Yes, by our enemies. I trust Lord Lakin to win it back."

"Good at cards is he then?"

"You bet."

"I'd rather not, if he's that good."

"Let us hope that he is, for if Surdin gain control of the Amulet, we are truly lost."

"For the moment then," said Daran, being practical, "let us fight this fight and do our part."

Erald clapped him on the back so hard that the dwarf fell over, and swore. Erald and Ben then approached the glowing, fiery Runesign, which hung in the air as if mocking them All right, then, it was mocking them. And why not? A central motif on the sign shimmered, then changed to a hand with one finger raised – and not in a gentlemanly salute. More of a rude retort, actually. Like Bunsen's Burner.

Erald and Ben strode out to confront the Runesign again. A curious collection of dwarfs followed at a discreet (i.e. safe) distance, to see if anything interesting, alarming (or best of all, amusing) happened to them. Erald drew his Golden Sword, and Ben pointed his staff, in what he believed to be a threatening gesture, throwing back his right hand in the traditional wizard's pose.

"Anyone got a camera for this one?" Ben called.

"Exposure problems. Needs about four light years at F8, and no one here's gone digital yet," was the reply.

"I dunno. Thought dwarfs were meant to be good at technology."

"Craftsmanship yes. Iron working, metal fabrication, yes: Zen Buddhism and the Art of Motorcycle Maintenance, yes: computers, no."

A sotto voice chorus added various other essential attributes, mainly drink related.

"Typical. The one time you want anything useful, and they can't do it," Ben complained.

"Just have to botch this one up on our own then, without professional help, won't we?" Erald answered.

"Yep. Let us enter our time of Persil."

"Shouldn't that be peril?"

"My underwear needs a clean."

Erald began chanting in a deep voice. The echoes ran around the chamber, looking for a way out. Finding none (except the fire exit, blocked by the Runesign, the echoes flashed into view as writhing coloured shapes, which changed hue and identity all the time. His sword took on a bright gleam of golden light, leaving retina patterns on the air as it was flourished, and reminded several watching of really bad tie-die tee shirts they had worn in the seventies.

Ben now joined the fun. His chant was in a minor key, forming a counterpoint to Erald's tone. The top of Ben's staff let forth a blaze of white light that became too bright for the watching dwarfs, who turned away. Erald never turned his gaze from the target, but reached out and hit Ben gently on the arm, to attract his attention. Unfortunately, he used the hand holding the sword.

"OW! Yer nearly had me arm off, yer bloody goon."

"Nevermind."

"Nirvana, here we come."

Together, the sword and staff thrust at the Runesign, which flared at once to three times its original size, shone like a veritable star fallen from the skies, then with an extremely rude noise it collapsed and vanished. Erald fell to the floor, unconscious.

Worried but elated, the dwarfs rushed over to the victorious pair. "Is he all right, Wizard?" they asked.

"He's away with the ferries."

"Don't you mean the fairies?"

"No. He prefers sailors."

Edchern marshalled his force.

"Where are you going?" asked Ben, as Erald shook his head, in an attempt to encourage the brain cells to communicate with each other.

Daran answered: "We are going to seek our revenge, have a good fight, and find the stock of beer we left in the Throne Room."

"Won't the Bodgandor have had that?"

"Nah, no taste. They only drink lager." All shuddered at the awful thought.

Edchern brandished his word above his head, and with fearful scowls, the dwarfs tramped off dawn the broad stairs. The Cavern was left in peace. Slowly, Erald sat upright.

"Did we defeat the Runesign?"

"Yes, my friend."

"Good. Then we can begin the fight to reclaim the Helvyndelve. Where have all the dwarfs gone?"

"To get a drink, and regain the Throne Room."

"Good. After that, we can seek out the Lower Deep, and then restore some of the lights. With the dwarfs there, too, we can marshal a force to sweep the Bodgandor out of the Delve. I am sure that the dwarfs lost the first fight only because they were taken by surprise."

"What of Ned?"

Erald sat very still, then floated gently to six inches above the floor, intoning his favourite mantra 'Talisker, Talisker' as he did so. The whisky failed to materialise (normally his prime objective), but he did become a little enlightened. It is almost impossible to achieve full enlightenment when you use whisky brands as a meditation mantra.

"Ned has left the Delve, taking the Amulet of Kings with him."

"The devil he has! What does he seek to do?"

"He should be taking it to his master, The Grey Mage, and that would be a grievous blow for us. With the power of the Amulet, the Grey Mage could rise to the top of the heap in Caer Surdin, and we know that he would drive the war against us harder than the present Dark Council do. This horde of Bodgandor are his doing, and he seeks advantage not only over us but also over his fellows by assaulting the Helvyndelve. Imagine their reaction should they return from abroad to find him the Master of Helvyndelve, and master of the Amulet of Kings."

"Right. So he's a social climber too."

"More like an antisocial climber."

"What do we do, Erald?"

"Nothing. We cannot catch Ned now. But I feel that he will not seek the Grey Mage, for if he, Ned, can attune to the Amulet himself, then he will have great power."

"Aye, an' he's an ambitious little git."

Erald resumed the lotus position, six inches above the floor. Well, it saved his clothes from getting dirty. More dirty. Or at least, more dirty than they were already. Enlightened magical beings often have trouble with the earth bound demonic forces contained within the average washer/drier. Especially the ones that come from Northern Italy, where the last process on leaving the factory is a mass exorcism by a catholic priest, in a desperate attempt to keep the electrics working until the warranty expires. His mantra was intoned again, and again, and again, until Ben poked Erald with his staff. The Tuatha emerged from his trance with a jolt, receiving a second jolt seconds later when he hit the floor.

"That was dangerous. It's like waking up a sleepwalker."

"Aye. I could see the resemblance. I thought you were asleep."

"I was meditating."

"And snoring."

"That was my mystical mantra."

"Snoring?"

"Works for me." *

*[And indeed for me too. And for you, if you try hard enough]

"Whatever."

"My spirit wandered and I have seen much."

"Yer got inside the brewery, then?"

Erald gave Ben a filthy look – almost, indeed, as filthy as his robes had become. "Small troops of Bodgandor are abroad."

"Better there than here, especially if they've gone off to Yorkshire. Might raise the tone."

"I mean that they roam the fells."

"I blame the Government. That Right to Roam were a disgrace. Only last month we woke up an' found the garden full of hikers, roaming. Hah! Grizelda soon sorted them out. Some of them still have to hop about on a wet morning, catching flies."

"Also, I saw the Grey Mage on Skiddaw, calling the Bodgandor to rally to him. Ned himself I could not spy, but I did see Dinas Tewet, and saw that someone has raised a Dark Mound at the Altar Stone."

"They're quite hard too. I read the instructions once, an' had to go for a pint to settle me nerves."

"Ben, anything is enough to make you want to go for a pint."

"Too right. In fact…"

"No."

"But…"

"No."

"Even the dwarfs have gone for a drink."

"They've got to fight through a bunch of teeming Bodgandor to get to the beer."

"Sounds like a fair deal to me."

"I could not spy Ned. It is in my thoughts that he has taken the Amulet himself into the Mound, to try to wrest control over the precious thing for himself."

"Aye. I could see him doing that," said Ben slowly. "He always was a greedy lad. Now I bet he's greedy for power. Did yer happen to see the kids at all?"

"No. Nor did I see Lakin or Fungus the BogTroll. But dwarfs, on guard, surrounded Dinas Tewet. I fear that they too may have entered the Mound, in pursuit perhaps of Ned?"

"Grizelda won't be happy about that."

"We cannot help that. And it was scarcely your fault."

"She won't stop to think about that. I'll get the blame as usual."

"Other fields I have seen too, and my brothers have sent me words I will not repeat yet.* Come, my friend, let's see what is happening with our battle," said Erald, changing the subject.

*[Come on. Got to keep the suspense going.]

Ben raised his staff high, and allowed radiance to flood the cavern. Apart from the bodies made earlier** there was little to be seen. Carefully they set off down the broad stairs leading to the Chamber of the Throne. More bodies lay scattered around at the bottom of the stairs, testament to the fierce defence the Bodgandor had mounted to protect their laager.*** And the lager too, of course.

** [By the fighting of course, not by Blue Peter presenters on holiday]

*** [A laager is where fighting soldiers can rest overnight, in a secure environment. Yes, and probably drink some lager too. If they have any.]

Entering the Chamber, the trail of bodies ran across the floor to the opposite Doors, now barred. On one side lay some dwarfs, who had fallen in the rush to the bar. Daran walked slowly towards the two, his sword uncleaned from the combat. His helm was missing, and a bandage covered one ear.

"What happened to your helmet?" asked Ben.

"Milim is using it to quaff the ale we recovered."

"Why doesn't he use his own?"

"With *his* hair? Ugh!"

Edchern joined them. "I have sent some to relieve the siege of the lower chambers, and the cavern of a Thousand Knights. Soon, we would hope to have retaken the whole of the Central Delve, and then our enemies will hold only the Northern Delve.

We will then look to throw them from our home."

Erald turned, and walked to the dais, standing beside the Throne he called for quiet in the Chamber. "Comrades!" he yelled at the dwarfs.

"Who's he think he is, Che Guavara?" Even amongst dwarfs, there is always one.

"Doesn't look like Che to me. Got a poster on me wall."

"That's Cher, you idiot. One's a singer, the other one's a freedom fighter." *

"What's the difference?"

"You can negotiate with a terrorist."

[* The difference between a terrorist and a freedom fighter usually depends on who wins.]

"The Central Delve is free, and the Bodgandor flee. But a greater menace has arisen." Declaimed Erald.

"Denis?" The above dwarf again.

"Who?"

"He was a menace."

"Shut up."

Erald glared at the dwarfs, and continued. "On top of Skiddaw, the Grey Mage is raising a last band of these Bodgandor, to sweep down the hills, backed by FireTrolls seeking revenge for their brothers. He seeks to drive us from these Halls, and take them for his own."

The dwarfs left Erald in no doubt that they thought the Grey Mage was biting off more than he could chew.

"He has brought enough of them over from their world to do this job for him. But to keep their loyalty, he will have to supply them with their needs. The Helvyndelve alone will not do that, so he seeks to overrun the whole of the Lakes with his army. The humans will be unable to stand before him. But the Edern will."

"The Edern?" came a voice from the crowd. Probably the famous A N Other Dwarf. "Where were they when we were attacked?"

"They had to fight an army themselves, that attacked them in Sinadon. But that they did, and they won. So now they come, riding to your aid in accordance with the ancient contract. (as amended, of course). The Grey Mage seeks to ambush them as they enter the Borrowdale. If the Grey Mage breaks the Edernhost, then his Bodgandor will boil through the King How Doors, and Helvyndelve will truly fall. We must join them and destroy this horde, that you are safe here."

"Their fate is not our fight," called one dwarf.

"Comrades, I appeal to you."

"I prefer Cher."

"Shuttup."

"Tuatha, you have fought with us, and we respect that," shouted a dwarf. "But by what right do you seek to command us?"

Erald paused, then reached inside his robes, and pulled out a large silver replica of the Amulet of Kings. There was a gasp from the dwarfs. "The last Archlord made me a Warden of the Delve before he vanished. I am the last living of the Wardens he made, and until another Archlord sits upon the Throne of Kings, I have Power within these Halls. The Steward was the only other Warden alive, and I would not have usurped his position. But he has fallen, and so I do command you to help."

The dwarfs went into a large huddle, and started arguing amongst themselves. It took some time for a consensus to emerge. At least one break for refreshments from the huge, but diminishing pile of cans in one corner of the Chamber was required. But at last, the dwarfs agreed. Daran was made spokesdwarf.

"The lads have agreed to follow you and fight as you direct. But in return..."

"Yes?"

"They want more beer and six hundred mixed pizza's from Barry's Pizza Parlour."

"Done." Erald turned to Ben, who looked a little confused. "I've had worse demands from my Brother Tuatha's in the past. At least this lot did not insist on spending a weekend in the pub. And on the credit cards, after the holiday kitty was used up. Had to call in a debt counsellor to sort it out, and the interest charges were murder."

Erald ordered the dwarfs to form up, and leaving a small guard in the Chamber of the Throne, led his troops off down the Western Passage.

"I remember when all this was shining with lights," said Daran, nostalgically.

"I dunno," said Ben. "Being here is like living in a timewarp." At once all the dwarfs jumped a pace to the left, and stepped back to the right. Ben turned round, his hands on his hips. "Are you lot taking the mickey, or what?"

"Sorry, just something we do."

As they marched down the passage, the dwarfs filled their time in the traditional manner of all soldiers. They sharpened their weapons, told dirty jokes and complained about the lack of food and the quality of the leadership. Dwarfs may have a reputation for being good with anything mechanical, but they are truly second to none in the art of complaining, and so were fully occupied. Ben however, was not so occupied, and hence filled his time by worrying.

"Don't worry so much," Erald advised him.

"Worrying works. 90% of the things I worry about never happen to me."

At length, the party reached the guard chambers by the Bowder Stone Doors. The small collection of guards there was very pleased to see them.

"What is happening outside?" Erald asked.

The guards looked at each other. "Dunno. Haven't looked. But nothing's tried to get in since you arrived."

"Right." Erald pushed passed the motley crew, and opened the Door a crack. Silently he slipped outside. Impatiently, the dwarfs awaited his return. At length he appeared at the barely open door, slid inside and closed the door.

"Well!" he exclaimed, "we are here in the nick of time. The EdernHost is entering the end of the valley, and Bodgandor on these hills are preparing an ambush. If we wait until they are ready, then we can ambush them as they prepare to strike. But be ready, for it is fully dark outside."

A fierce growl from the dwarfs showed that they approved of the plan. Erald went back outside, hiding below the Bowder Stone itself, and watching carefully. With bright banners flying in the starlight, the Edernhost rode carefully into the valley floor, with lone scouts riding before them, and on either side. As the vanguard turned into the valley at Rosthwaite, the Bodgandor gave a great shout and released a storm of arrows upon them, before running down the slopes of the valley, to attack.

Erald threw back his cloak and drew the golden sword. The Doors vanished before him, and with a loud shout, the dwarf army followed him.

Chapter Twelve

Malan and Lugh were picking up the kitchen table, disturbing the goat, which had sheltered beneath it. In revenge, the goat's various stomachs made disturbing noises.

"Don't light any matches," Lugh warned.

The two Tuatha jammed the table against the kitchen door, which was splintered and cracked, the bolts no longer firmly attached. Behind them, the goat investigated the Bodgandor curry, and with little regard for its personal safety, started eating. Malan looked out of the kitchen window, drawing back as an arrow passed swiftly through the frame, showering him with glass. Grizelda screeched in fury.

"That was Pilkington's self cleaning Glazing!" she fumed. "It's more expensive than gold!" She stuck her head out of the now very open window, and screamed a curse. The guilty Bodgandor, identified by his bow and a large smirk, doubled over. Lugh pulled her away from the window, just as two more arrows flew in. One skidded across the stone floor and went under the Welsh Dresser where it neatly skewered a rat. The other slammed into the door of the fridge, and stuck fast.

Once nominally white, the fridge now became a sort of burnt hombre, or dull orange for those of you reading in black and white. Grizelda and the two Tuatha backed away from it, whilst the goat continued slurping its way through the curry.

"Quick!" gasped Grizelda. "Open the door."

Malan shoved the table out of the way, and the fridge scraped and lurched its way through the door, and down the path into the garden. The sounds of fear and fighting grew loud, then lessened as the fridge made its presence felt. Also making its presence felt was the goat.

"What's that smell?" asked Lugh.

Grizelda did not answer. She was at the window, now in safety, for those Bodgandor who had not vanished into the freezer compartment or been trampled underfoot, had left quickly. The FireTroll however was battling furiously now, throwing firebolts and hitting at the waving fridge door with its sword. Malan grinned maliciously, and lit a match.

A moment later, the FireTroll was hit and bested by a ballistic goat, which went straight on through the remains of the garden gate, and slid to a halt besides an old garage fortunately made from asbestos panels (now banned on health grounds, rather like Grizelda's Bodgandor Curry. She has had to diversify into chilli instead). The FireTroll tried to get to its feet, failed, and as the fridge approached, fell back into the waiting freezer compartment. The door slammed shut, and the fridge began to resume its normal colour.

"Handy item, that" observed Malan.

"Dangerous though," said Lugh.

"It is quite fuel efficient." Grizelda defended the fridge, as it rocked past them back to its accustomed spot in the kitchen. "And I can't wait to see what's available in there tomorrow."

The two Tuatha decided that they could wait a very long time indeed. Lugh wandered over to see how much damage had been caused to the garage by the goat.

"Wow!" he breathed, looking through the window at Fungus's motorcycle. "It's a Harley!"

"Oh no, now we've lost him for half an hour," complained Malan.

"Fungus is the same. He can spend hours in there, getting it to work right. I keep telling him that that's what magic was invented for, but he say's I've got no soul," Grizelda told him.

Lugh was enthusing about the bike in a long monotone, but the others ignored him.

"Come an' have some tea," Grizelda invited.

"I don't fancy the curry."

"I don't think that the goat left any. I'll get the kettle on."

"OK. But we need to keep a look out for the EdernHost. They are riding to this battle, to help free the Helvyndelve from the danger that besets it. We hope that they will be here before too long, and our brothers with them."

"If that Finn's with them I'll need a few minutes to hide the drink." Grizelda turned to the large array of bottles on the dresser.

"I'll help. I could do with hiding a few drinks myself. That goat was only six inches from my nose when it took off."

"Shame about my garden. Scum have ruined it. You'd think that they came from Liverpool, and weren't used to growing things."

"I thought that they grew lots of plants in Liverpool."

"All the same variety, though."

"Ah. Right."

Malan put the kitchen table back in place, and went outside to pull a very reluctant Lugh into the kitchen for some refreshments. Grizelda put the teapot, and some unbroken mugs onto one end of the table, and then lay her broomstick on the other end. Opening a draw in the dresser, she pulled out a pot of sparkly blue paint and a narrow paintbrush. The Tuatha watched as she carefully started painting blue stripes along the side of the broom.

"What are they?"

"Go faster stripes. Guess what they do?"

Lakin stood at the entrance to the Dark Mound, his face grim. "They have taken the Amulet inside, and I must follow them. I cannot bid any to come with me, for this leads to Mortal Peril."

"I'm coming," said Linda, her face resolute. A fiery spirit had been awoken in her.

"Me too," said Chris. He was no resolute, but did not intend to listen to his sister telling him he was a wimp for the rest of their lives.

"You don't have to," Fungus told them.

"No, *you* don't have to," Linda replied.

"Are you joking? If I stayed out here, yer aunt would never forgive me. An' if I've got to go, then Haemar's coming too."

"Why?"

"Because no one will believe my boasting when we get back, otherwise."

"No one will believe you anyway," Haemar told him. "They never do."

As soon as the small party entered the Mound, darkness fell upon them. A thick, inky blackness, impenetrable and as beyond human understanding as the terms and conditions of a credit card company. Lakin stumbled, as he found the stairway. But seeing well in the dark, Haemar caught his belt and steadied him.

"We could do with some light," Haemar observed.

Chris held up his Ward, and a faint glow came from the silver charm. He was a bit disappointed.

"Here, other powers are subdued," Lakin told him. "But that will be enough for us to see by. Come!"

They began to descend the stairs, and at once a flight of bats (out of hell?) fell about their shoulders. Linda shrieked even more loudly than the bats. Lakin cut at them with his sword, but they only vanished when Chris waved his Ward at them.

"Remember!" ordered Lakin. "Nothing truly exists in this place."

"Except Death," Fungus reminded him.

"Well, yes, all right."

"Well, that's one thing then. What else?"

"How about that snake?" asked Haemar.

A huge Cobra rose from the floor in front of them, spitting venom at Haemar. Some landed on his armour, and ran off hissing (probably in disgust at the etchings). Lakin strode forward, unafraid, and the cobra vanished. "See? Illusion!"

The stairs led further down, to a landing. Here, a deep pool of water covered all but a narrow strip of stone along one wall. Haemar stepped confidently into the water, and then leapt back out with an agonised expression, a loud yell, and a very fierce fish fastened to his foot.

"An Illusion!" repeated Lakin.

Haemar repeated some phrases the teenagers should not really have known, whilst he flailed around trying to beat the fish off his foot. Finally the pesky piscine lost its grip, and fell back into the water leaving some very deep teeth marks in Haemar's left boot. They all crowded around to look.

"Teeth must be made of diamonds!" said Fungus, awed. Haemar pulled a fishing rod out of his pack, and cast the line into the pool. At once a fish that seemed to be mostly teeth ate its way up the line, and was starting on the end of the fishing rod when Haemar quickly threw what was left into the pool.

"You don't need a rod," Chris told him. "Just put your foot in it, and pull one out."

"Think I'll pass," Haemar answered.

"Illusion!" said Lakin fiercely, and strode across the water without incident.

Linda threw back her shoulders, and marched after him without problems. The rest of the party gawped at her with admiration, but failed to follow her example.

"I'm getting tired of him saying that all the time." Fungus grumbled, but put his foot tentatively into the pool. Several v shaped ripples on the water headed for his foot at some speed, and he quickly withdrew. Gingerly, they crept and shuffled along the narrow stone edge of the pool until they stood at the other side, besides a clearly exasperated Lakin, and a rather smug Linda. Lakin turned, and went on down the stairs. The dispirited party shuffled after him.

"How come he did that, an' we couldn't?" asked Haemar.

"Positive thinking," called back Lakin.

A little further, they halted at the next obstacle. A grey robed hermetic figure, whose cowl obscured the face completely, barred the stairs. It held a long staff in one hand, and a lantern in the other. Lakin walked straight at the hermit, but the arm holding the lantern was raised before his face, and he stopped.

"Are you thinking positive?" asked Haemar, who was still limping. And squelching from the water that had entered his boot through the teeth holes.

Lakin tried again, but again rebounded. "This is the last trial," he told them. "Once past the Hermit, we can follow Ned without hindrance."

Linda walked forward, and raised her Ward high. The Hermit

swivelled to face her. All right, it did not have a face (which makes fasting easy as a hermit), but there was no doubt she had its full attention. The Ward blazed with a sudden emerald light, outshining the grey hue of the Hermit, which bowed and vanished before her.

"Nice one!" applauded Chris.

"The stairs now lead to a side chamber, with a stone Altar. Probably that is where we will find Ned. If not, he will have gone on past the Temple to the Shore itself," Lakin told them.

"How do you know all this?" asked Linda.

"Good question," approved Fungus.

"Erald of the Tuatha brought me to this place once, some years back on an errand I will not talk about now, He brought me safely through these perils, and out again."

"Shame he is not with us now."

The stairs led down now only a short distance until a side passage loomed out of the dim glow from the ward held by Chris. The Archway entrance looked gloomy and forbidding. The design specification had insisted on an appearance that would deter any but the most determined entrant. Only those capable of showing the grit, resolve, patience and persistence required to obtain a sensible answer from the National Rail Enquiries Telephone Service were likely to succeed.

Lakin clearly had these qualities, for he had travelled widely on the national rail network (using a borrowed student railcard) but they were not widely shared by his colleagues.

"You mean we have to go in there?" asked Haemar.

The light around them grew dim as Chris regarded the dread portal. He could see two sets of footprints in the dust leading into the passageway.

"I guess so," muttered Fungus, with a marked lack of enthusiasm.

"Our best weapon is surprise," hissed Lakin.

"What about fear?" Haemar asked.

"All right, fear and surprise."

"You're not meant to use them on me."

"Follow me." ordered Lakin, and set off down the passage. Slowly, with varied degrees of enthusiasm (Haemar would have registered a negative had a hand held measuring device been available) they followed.

The Edernhost drew to a halt as they reached the mouth of the Borrowdale.

"What was that lake we just passed?"

"Wast Water," said Hankey, after a surreptitious look at the map on his mobile.

"Why is it called that?"

"Suppose they can't find a use for it."

"Has anyone been here before?" called Blear. "We need to calculate the optimum route to the Doors of the Helvyndelve."

There were no takers for the offer to become the scapegoat for not finding the best route.

"There will be a bonus, and a promotion available," he tempted. Still no one from the ranks stepped forward to offer advice.

"How about some Share Options?" There was a ripple of interest, but again the appeal was in vain.

Blear was disappointed, and expressed his feelings appropriately. "I might have to consider a corporate reconstruction when we get back," he threatened.

"Does he mean a Phoenix?" asked Hankey, who was still suffering from a painful wound acquired somewhere unmentionable when he fell off his horse on the journey, and accordingly was not entirely up to speed with developments.

"I thought that that was a bird," said Meillar.

"A myth," added Telem.

"Blear's miffed," Meillar added.

"A phoenix is a (now illegal) device for avoiding paying your bills." Hankey explained to the other two, who knew that anyway and were just taking the myth.

"Blear has been doing that for years. I lent him twenty quid last year, never got it back. He's been avoiding me since then, but I didn't know it was illegal."

"That's not illegal, just normal behaviour in a CEO."

Blear tired of receiving no roadside assistance. That was entirely his fault though, for forgetting to pay the renewal premiums. Besides, anyone who has had to wait for Roadside Assistance in the South Lakes knows just how long an hour's response time can stretch. Some claim that the motoring associations have done a deal with the technical team behind Doctor Who to manipulate real-time to fit in with their Terms and Conditions, but it has never been proved. The customer who wrote to the Times saying he had found the evidence mysteriously vanished, to reappear thirty years later with a memory lapse and a tendency to sleepwalk on motorways.

"What does your SatNav say, Hankey?"

"Get Lost."

"What!"

"That's what it says. The Helvyndelve is not programmed into the memory, and doesn't appear on the monthly updates."

"That's what comes of keeping it a secret dwelling for the dwarfs, instead of a tourist attraction, as we advised them a couple of years ago. With the sale of a few catering concessions, they could have cleaned up."

"The fact that they had to clean up first put them off, I think."

Blear, having run out of options, (the share options remained unissued), set scouts to ride in front and on the outskirts of the host, and waved the advance. Cautiously, they rode forward. The scouts, concentrating on picking their way forward missed the fleeting shapes of the Bodgandor, as they withdrew back before the advance.

The riders spread out as the valley floor widened. Knowing that the Doors of the Dwarfs were close, the Edern tensed, awaiting attack. It was not long before their fears were realised, as a storm of arrows fell from the slopes high above them.

"Ride for the trees!" yelled Blear, anxious to avoid losing his troops to arrows. The Edern scattered, heading for the trees that lay on either side of the valley, and ahead of them. Within a moment, the disciplined formation had been reduced to separate small groups of mounted Edern, seeking to avoid the arrows that still fell like rain. Any walker who has encountered a proper rainstorm in the North or the Lakes (unlike the gentle showers that fall on the soft southerners) will understand the reference. The hardy folk who hill walk in Wales would probably have shrugged off the arrow storm as a bit of light drizzle, barely worth a mention down the pub.

The Grey Mage had planned the ambush after an evening reading military history. He had almost had a heart attack from laughing, and had seriously contemplated going to a hospital, but settled for a stiff whisky instead on the grounds that it was probably more effective than most of the NHS treatments. Except those which they keep for politicians and their own staff, of course.

Accordingly, with so many examples of what not to do laid before him (The Charge of the Light Brigade in particular had almost finished him off he had laughed so much, with Marshall Ney at Waterloo coming a close second)* he had managed to create complete chaos in his enemy before sending the Bodgandor down at them. Without hesitation, he gave his orders.

* [Two perfect examples of how some military men find bravery and complete stupidity interchangeable terms]

The trees and slopes of the valley sides suddenly sprouted yelling Bodgandor who lost no time in falling on the confused and scattered Edern. Blear swiftly realised that he had lost control of the situation at micro level. He too had studied much military history, although with less attention to detail and had crucially not undertaken a holistic view of each of the famous engagements he had studied. One fact he had gleaned from reading about World War One was that staff officers functioned best when able to take an overview of events in order to take strategic decisions. (i.e. to avoid being involved in any of the actual fighting, but to observe from a safe distance) and accordingly he galloped for the slopes nearest to him.

Telem and Hankey watched him go.

"Our glorious leader seems to be leaving the fray," observed Telem, casually chopping the heads off two Bodgandor who had closed upon him with threatening swords and rude insults.

"I will expect a sharply worded memo to arrive in due course," replied Hankey, burying his spear to the hilt in a passing Bodgandor, who passed on.

"The pen is mightier than the sword," quoted Telem.

Hankey drew a pen from his pocket, and threw it towards a large Bodgandor chief that was creeping up behind Telem, with evil intentions. The Bodgandor paused to chop the pen in half with his sword, in mid air.

"Don't see that one, myself." Hankey then treated the distracted Bodgandor to a vicious spear thrust.

Upon the slopes of High Spy, the Grey Mage (who had also read a lot of World War One history and in fact agreed with several of Lord Blear's conclusions, which only goes to show) grinned to see his plan working so well. The Edern had not been outnumbered, but had been first disordered and then assaulted. "Goes to show," he muttered to himself. "If Generals had grown up on the football terraces instead of playing cricket, most wars would have been shorter."

He raised an arm, and sent an orange flare across the valley. On the far side, waited one of the Watches, as his sub commander. This trainee warlock had been press ganged out of his taxi to help, because most taxi drivers know how to fight dirty. If you want to road test this theory, take a long drive and tell the driver at the other end you haven't any cash. But do not blame me for what happens next. The watching Watcher saw the signal and sent the reserves of Bodgandor down into the valley.

But also watching, as we have seen was Erald. He opened the Doors of the Helvyndelve, and the dwarfs who were filled with a righteous anger at the invasion of their home, and the theft of their beer supply, (not necessarily in that order) swarmed down the hillsides in pursuit. Erald followed, his golden sword gleaming in the dusk.

The dwarfs yelled their traditional war cry.*

[* We've done that one already. I didn't think it was good enough for a repeat performance.]

"Havoc!" yelled some traditionalists.

"We're missing last orders!" yelled others.

"Leave some for me!"

"They won't like it up 'em!"

In the valley floor, Telem and Hankey had been struggling to draw together their forces to create a co-coordinated defence. Not having been to a military college, or read any of the memoirs or appreciations of the world's great generals, they were relying upon a blend of innate intelligence and common sense, and as a result managing quite well.

In fact, they were well able to appreciate the effect on their foes of the unexpected arrival of the dwarfs in the Bodgandor's rear (so to speak). Indeed, the spears and swords of the dwarfs soon made a difference, and the tide of battle began to turn.

On the valley side below the Bowder Stone, Ben had not followed the dwarfs into combat. Not because he was a World War One student, but because he had spied the black cowled shape on the slopes, and recognised him. Not a bad trick, when all that was visible was a black hood and cloak, with a short black stick sticking (as it were) out of one long sleeve. Accordingly he moved quickly across the slope to cause a confrontation.

"OI! You!"

"Me?"

"I've seen you before, haven't I?"

"Me? Don't think so."

"Yes I have. You were with that Ned when he had a go at me an' the wife in our cottage. One of them Watches, aren't yer?"

"I thought you were still in the cottage. Boss said you were finished."

"Why was that then?"

"He sent a FireTroll and a shed load of Bodgandor to finish you off."

Ben went white. "Grizelda were there on her own," he said, slowly.

"Can she cope with a FireTroll, on her own?" asked the apprentice wizard.

"She's always managed against you lot OK, with or without me."

"But a FireTroll?"

"She got rid of a Taxman!" declaimed Ben, now seriously concerned but determined not to show it.

"Yes, I heard about that. Wasn't there, because I was on shift at the time."

"You were lucky then."

"Yes, cos I got a good wedding party and made a mint out of the tips. Couple more an' I could afford to pay me own way to the conference next year. Hope its still somewhere warm."

"Don't be worried about that, cos I'm going to send you somewhere warm now."

"I can't afford Greece at the moment."

"Wasn't thinking of Greece."

"Can't abide Spain."

"How about Hell?"

"Don't think they do packages yet. Do Virgin fly there then?"

"Let's find out." Ben aimed his staff at the Watcher, and a blast of white light (and white heat) shot at the other, who swirled his cloak and absorbed the blast.

"Where did yer get that cloak then?"

"Mail order. Boss got us a job lot, like the staffs." The black-cowled one brandished his small staff.

"You've only got a small one, then."

"Don't be so personal. I had a bigger one, but it got eaten."

"By what? Or Who? If that's not too personal."

"By a yoghurt from your fridge. One of those kids threw it at Ned, an' it got my staff instead."

"Pity."

"Yes. It cost me two weeks wages."

"No, I meant it were a pity it missed Ned."

"Oh well, you can't have everything. Try having this one."

The small staff spun, and a black mist formed in the air, and tried to envelope Ben. But Ben spun his own staff, and the staff sucked the black mist out of the air, and swallowed it.

"Hey, that stuff's not cheap either!"

Ben's wrists twisted, and the end of his staff flicked out and caught the other a right ding on the side of the head. Why a ding? Well, that was the sound it made on impact.

"Ouch! That's cheating!" Ben's opponent then spread his arms, and (with no small resemblance to a seagull that had been sprayed black by a passing Goth with no sentiment for wildlife) began chanting some mystic runes. Ben allowed his attention to wander, and his eyes went wide as he looked out across the valley floor at a veritable flood of Bodgandor howling down from the Honister Pass to join the battle. Up the slope towards him climbed (puffing a bit for climbing steep hills is not normally on the evil warlock recruiting posters) came two more of the Watches, to their fellow's aid.

*

Back at the cottage, Malan was beginning to relax after his third cup of tea, and a full packet of chocolate digestives.

"Is there any more tea in the pot?" he asked.

"Guess I could squeeze one out," replied the teapot, sucking in its sides as it spoke.

However, at that moment came a thunderous knocking at the remains of the front door. All three looked at each other.

"Not again," groaned Lugh.

"Is there anybody there?" called a voice from outside.

"No, the place is empty," called back Grizelda.

There was a moment of silence. "Finn, I don't understand. If there's no one there, who answered me?"

"It's a witch's cottage, Diarmid. She's probably got an answering service."

"Like you get from BT on 1571?"

"Probably works better. And probably got some additional features not offered by a phone company."

"Such as?"

"Well, one witch I knew bought this add on, that asked the caller twenty questions. If they got any of them wrong, her knocker turned into a dragon's head and fried the caller where they stood."

"Bet that was awkward for her husband."

"Her door knocker, idiot."

Lugh and Malan looked at each other in relief. Grizelda looked as though she would rather the FireTroll was back.

"Let them in," she groaned, and put the kettle back on the hob.

Lugh opened the door, and Laeg, Finn, Liamm and Diarmid came into the cottage, and looked around.

"Been redecorating?" Laeg asked. "No good asking these two to help."

"Actually," Malan retorted, "we helped save Grizelda's life when the cottage was attacked by a storm of Bodgandor, and a FireTroll."

"So what happened to the FireTroll?" asked Finn.

Malan pointed to the fridge, which made a happy burping sound. Everyone took a pace back away from it, except Grizelda, who opened the fridge door. The Tuatha all took a further step back, but all that could be seen in the fridge were several rows of brick red yoghurt pots and a bottle of milk. Grizelda sneered at the Tuatha, and took the milk out of the fridge, and put it on the table with several mugs, another packet of biscuits and a rejuvenated (and fatter) teapot. Grizelda put the protesting kettle back on the hob.

"OK," said Lugh, through a mouthful of chocolate digestive, "what's the news?"

"Well," replied Laeg, "we came out of Sinadon with the Edernhost. Telem had been fighting on the beaches already, so we were able to cross to the mainland quite easily, and ride for the Helvyndelve."

"No trouble?"

"I nearly thumped Blear a couple of times," said Liamm.

"With the Bodgandor, I meant."

"Oh, them, not really. So when we got close to here, we left the Edern to get to the Helvyndelve, and came to see if you lot were OK. Erald had sent word that you might need some help."

"Not us."

The kettle started to boil, and as the steam issued from the spout, it turned into a close representation of Erald's head. Facing the wrong way, of course. "Blast." The steam head said to the blank wall, and turned around to face the room.

"Hey look," Diarmid said. "The steam looks like Erald."

"Nah, it's just a co incidence, like that Turin Shroud thing."

"I though that that was a forgery."

"Maybe this Erald head is a forgery."

"Who would bother?"

"I'd get more sense from the blank wall," grumbled Erald, turning to look at Grizelda.

"Are you OK, then?" he asked. "Ben was worried."

"Is he OK?"

"Fine."

"What about my wards?"

"They were taken by those kids you had here."

"It was the kids I meant, idiot."

"Oh. Well, I don't know, they went off with Lakin, and even I cannot see them at the moment. I will let you know if I do."

"Best you do."

"Promise. Now, are my lot all here?"

"Unless there are a few more of them in the woodshed. But as I put the chocolate biccies out, I've probably collected a full set."

"Then you are probably due a consolation prize. Anyway, Laeg, can you hear me?"

"Yes, Erald."

"Are the others sober?"

"They do impressions."

"Well get over here as fast as you can. The Edernhost has ridden into a trap at Rosthwaite, and even with these dwarfs here we need all the help that we can get. Grizelda, we could use you too, as the Grey Mage has his Watches here, and Ben is having a hard time on his own."

"OK, Erald. We are on the way," said Lugh, jumping up.

"How far is it to this place?"

"Half an hour for you lot to walk," answered Grizelda, picking up her broomstick.

"Suppose its no good asking you for a lift?" asked Finn, hopefully.

"Not a chance." Grizelda strode to the door. "Are you lot coming, then?"

"I've got an idea." Said Lugh, slowly.

"Bet it feels lonely, in there."

"We'll nick Fungus's motorbike."

"That's not a bad idea."

The Tuatha all hurried out to the garage, Grizelda protesting behind them. Lugh opened the doors, and found not only the

Harley, but also a beautiful Triumph Bonneville, He gasped in awe, and walked reverently up to the Bonnie.

"It's the American export model. Wherever did he get it from?"

"You know Fungus," said Grizelda. "Traded it for a spare microphone he had lying around. I think it works."

Lugh found that the keys were in both bikes, and grasping the Bonnie put his foot on the kick start, gasping in shock a moment later as the kick-start kicked back and scraped painfully up the inside of his right leg. Malan sniggered.

"Fungus said it always did that to him, too, so he installed an optional extra." Grizelda told Lugh, as he hopped round on one leg. She reached out and tapped the engine block with her right forefinger. At once the engine burst into life. The Harley of course just turned over on the key, which was less impressive but more useful.

"Now we'll get there on time," enthused Lugh. Less enthusiastically, for they had experienced his riding before, the rest of the Tuatha selected their travelling companions. After a brief struggle, Finn ended up behind Lugh, whilst Laeg drove the Harley with Malan and Diarmid sharing the pillion set. Uncomfortable, even on a Harley, but better than being behind Lugh they agreed. Carefully, they drove out of the garage, whilst Grizelda started her broomstick, and wobbled slowly upwards. Neither Finn nor Lugh saw her point her finger at the Bonneville, and mutter a complicated spell.

Malan did, though. "What was that?" he asked. "A spell to make it go faster?"

"Sort of. I just disabled the brakes."

"Aren't you going to tell them?"

"I think we'll let them find out for themselves."

Malan opened his mouth to argue (against his better judgement) but all he received in return was a mouth full of exhaust smoke as the Bonnie went through the garden gate in a screaming powerslide, Lugh whooping with delight.

Lugh roared up the lane, with the Harley following and Grizelda keeping station above them. The ill assorted trio soon found themselves slowing down, as the bikes climbed their way up the Honister Pass. At the top, they coasted to a halt and looked down the pass. At first the road seemed clear, then as if by magic, files of Bodgandor appeared through the dusk, blocking their way. The faces of the Tuatha grew grim (and in the case of those on the Harley a little grey from the Bonnie's exhaust fumes). Finn drew his sword, and Moran and Diarmid readied their spears. Then with a howl, they gunned the motorcycles down the hill at the Bodgandor. Grizelda too attacked, firing yellow hexes in all directions.

The Bodgandor broke, and fled back down the pass into the valley, where their fellows still battled with the Edernhost. Grizelda spotted Ben on the far side of the valley, doing battle with three opponents. She screamed a curse (which missed) and shot across the valley floor at almost thirty feet, scaring the Edern's horses, terrifying Bodgandor and causing mayhem by her passage.

The Bodgandor driven down the pass turned as they met their compatriots, but scattered and fled or fell as, with a dreadful scream of tortured metal (Lugh had selected the wrong gear – again) the Bonneville barrelled into the fight, Finn entering into the spirit of the fray by grabbing Lugh's sword in his other hand and sticking both swords out sideways in hope. He had once seen the statue of Boudicca's chariot in London, with the twin, wheel mounted scythes, and had been jealous ever since. Now he smiled as widely as Lugh. Leaning so far over that the footrests scraped the ground, Lugh and Finn cut through the Bodgandor, causing mayhem and casualties.

But Lugh's smile turned to a rictus of horror as he discovered just how Grizelda had helped. "The brakes don't work!" he yelled back at Finn.

"You what?"

"I can't make the brakes work!"

"Do you want me to have a go?"

"Don't be stupid, we can't swap places on a motorcycle doing 60mph."

"Tom Cruise managed it in that film, and he did all his own stunts."

"Maybe, but I'm not trying it, at least not unless Cameron Diaz is on the back instead of you."

The Bonneville, now almost entirely out of control, cut a swathe through a last group of Bodgandor who had been facing the other way, cannoned off a low wall, stalled, and fell over, very slowly.

Lugh staggered to his feet. "That went well."

Incoherent sounds from beside, and largely underneath, the rather hot motorcycle disagreed with him. Lugh removed a spare Bodgandor head from the headlight. At least Lugh considered the head spare; its original owner had probably had different views on the subject but was no longer able to express them. Finn was becoming able to express his views. Extricating himself, with no little difficulty from underneath the Bonneville, he started cursing Lugh. As the volume and complexity of the invective grew, the few remaining skirmishes stopped as both Edern and Bodgandor stopped to listen, and in some cases applaud or take notes.

The abuse even drifted as far up the hillside as Ben and Grizelda. Grizelda had defeated two of Ben's opponents by the simple strategy of crash landing on them, and as they lay under the remains of her broomstick, picking bits of bristle and twig from sensitive areas of their anatomy they could only agree with the sentiments Finn was expressing. The third had taken advantage of the distraction to simply run away.

"Was that your fault?" asked Ben accusingly, looking down at the Bonneville created devastation below.

"Of course not. Well, I did hex the brakes a bit, but they didn't need to arrive that fast. Look, there's the Harley coming, there's no problems there."

"The Harley as well? Fungus is going to kill you."

"I'll make it up to him. Bake him a cake, or something."

"It'll take a bit more than a cake."

"I know, Ben, when we've won, he can use the garden for a victory concert."

"Actually, that's not a bad idea. It's ages since we went

dancing."

"I'll dance on your grave, when I've finally decided to let you off the hook and be killed!" came faintly up the slope, as Finn continued.

Further across the valley, the Harley was now making a more stately and dignified entrance, but the Bodgandor had had enough. Leaving the Edern, they started to withdraw across the valley towards Castle Crag and the Grey Mage.

"Reinforcements I need," muttered the warlock, as he watched his defeated Bodgandor gather together at the foot of the hill. But he had no more to send.

"Where's that dratted Ned, I wonder? If he had brought me the Amulet, as we arranged, I could bring enough Bodgandor here in minutes to overrun that lot."

Indeed, the armies of both the Edern and the dwarfs were clearly weary, despite having defeated and slain vast numbers of their foes. Bodgandor bodies (and arms, legs and heads) lay scattered widely over the battleground. Telem and Hankey were trying to rouse the Edern to attack their demoralised foes, and Blear had returned and was haranguing everyone within earshot.

The Tuatha had gathered together, and were now calming Finn down, with an emergency whisky bottle Malan just happened to be carrying. The dwarfs were scavenging the battlefield for valuable metals or minerals that could be recycled. It was clear that the battle was nearly over.

The Grey Mage collected his picked Bodgandor Guard, and set off at a fast jog towards his waiting taxi. He was heading for

Dinas Tewet, to see for himself what was happening.

*

Ned stood at the Stone Altar, holding the Amulet of Kings, and in deep thought. The only light in the chamber came from the glow cast by the FireTroll. The chamber was round, with a huge but unadorned Stone Altar standing in the centre. Beyond the Altar, two more passages left the chamber, one leading up and one leading downwards.

Cautiously, Lakin peered around the edge of the tunnel leading into the Chamber. He waved an arm back as a signal to his small band to keep quiet and press back against the tunnel wall. They all drew their swords, and deep breaths. The thin grey light from the Ward of Lingard held by Chris flickered and went out, leaving only the faint green glow from Fungus as illumination.

"I feel sick," Haemar whispered to Fungus.

"Good. We could do with the colour round here."

Lakin waved them to silence, peering again around the corner of the tunnel.

Ned stood before the Altar, with both arms raised. He had in front of him a small notebook and the Amulet itself lay in the very centre of the Altar. As Lakin watched, Ned lowered his arms, and made a gesture with them across the Altar. A cloud of smoke so black that it could be seen even against the darkened walls of the ill lit Chamber, arose from one end of the Altar and formed an unpleasant shape, complete with eyes.

The chant resumed, and the echoes (who didn't fancy being near the cloud) ran quickly around the Chamber and down the tunnel to get out.

"What's going on?" asked Linda, with some bravado.

"I think that Ned has failed to gain control over the Amulet, and so he has summoned a demonic entity to aid him. But this is dangerous, and may turn against him for demons delight in deceit and entrapment. However, there is a chance that he might succeed, so I must interfere."

Lakin paused, clearly awaiting a chorus of concern. Such was not forthcoming. "Fungus," he hissed.

"Yeah?"

"You're coming with me."

"Not if you are contemplating something dangerous."

"Fungus, we are in an eldritch Dark Mound, which strictly speaking does not exist in our world. How much danger do you not want to be in? Do you want to bring your charges safely back to Grotbags?"

"Ah. Threats. You know where you are with threats. I suppose that I don't have much choice, do I?"

"Not really, no. Your job will be to occupy the FireTroll and the demon, whilst I sort out Ned."

"Basically, to be fried by one of them, and eaten by the other. Do I look like fast food?"

"Fungus, you've never been fast at anything."

"I was pretty fast at that gig near Leeds."

"Only," contributed Haemar, "because the promoter was running away with the takings."

Linda pushed forward, energised by the mention of fast food. "I'm coming too. My Ward has started glowing, so I think it wants to do something."

Lakin looked at her. "Sorry, but it is too dangerous."

"I'm not listening to that. My Ward wants to help."

"Well, it is true that the Wards bear the same source roots of magic as this Mound, and for that matter, the demon. Stay close to the tunnel wall, and let 's see."

Lakin drew himself up to his full four feet of height, and sprang out into the Chamber, Fungus following less enthusiastically. Linda peered around the corner at them.

"Not you again," complained Ned. "You crop up like house music at a disco."

"And you've brought a pet with you. I can smell it from here," sneered the FireTroll. "Don't forget that peat burns well."

"Who's Pete?" asked Lakin.

"Steady on," warned Fungus. "As a BogTroll I have many mystical powers."

"Name one."

"I can make Acid Rain."

"Nah, everyone knows that's caused by Swedish Power

stations."

"I thought it were rain forests?" queried Ned.

"Actually, it's the amount he drinks in the Red Lion," said Lakin.

"The beer there has the same effect on me." Ned sighed.

"Try another one," suggested the FireTroll, moving round the Altar. Lakin slid away from Fungus towards Ned, who didn't notice. Fungus did notice, and treated Lakin to a reproachful stare.

"I don't burn well," warned Fungus, watching the FireTroll carefully.

"Oh, you wouldn't be for me, but for my friend here."

"We haven't been introduced. It wouldn't be good manners to feed me to something you hadn't introduced me to."

"This is the Demon Melgior. Melgior, this is lunch. There, that's the formalities over."

The FireTroll flicked a wrist, and a small fireball appeared, and flew at Fungus who ducked. A second and third set of fireballs flew within moments. The latter made an impact, but promptly fizzled out. Fungus flicked his own wrist in the same way, and a damp, green ball flew across the room to land squarely on the FireTroll's chest. There was a huge burst of steam, and the FireTroll stepped smartly backwards. The burning red colour had left its chest, which was now a dark black colour.

"Your lunch, you cook it." The FireTroll muttered to the demon.

"Right. Little BogTroll." The demon cloud grew larger, and roiled around the Altar towards Fungus.

"Frodo Lives, says your cap, but your time has come. I'll nick that cap, then eat what's left."

"You can't eat me. I'm a musician."

The black cloud stopped abruptly. "Is that right? What do you play?"

"Blues and jazz, mostly."

"I meant, what instrument?"

"Sax." Fungus pulled his battered sax around from his back, and offered it for inspection.

"I'm on vibraphones for the house band."

"That's cool."

"Instead of eating you, I think..."

"Yes?" said Fungus, hopefully.

"I'll just drag you down to the Seventh Circle of Hell with me and you can join the band."

"Do you mind if I pass?"

"Let's hear you play first."

Fungus took a deep breath, and launched into *Strangers on the Shore*.

"Nah, I can't eat someone who can play like that. Come on, let's go for the gig," said the demon.

Fungus backed off. "I'm too young to go."

"What do you mean? As a BogTroll, your age changes all the time."

"Doesn't everyone's?"

Linda felt a jolt through her body, and looking down saw that the Ward around her neck was glowing bright green. A word was forming on the silver necklet, and without thinking she spoke it aloud. "Habitatawaymus."

The demon screamed, causing all there to put their hands over their ears. Then golden chains appeared in mid air, and wrapped themselves tightly around the black cloud, even as it reached out for Fungus. The chains grew tighter, and then with a wail, the demon vanished. The FireTroll, whose chest had still not relit, turned and lumbered at its best speed through the right hand tunnel behind the Altar.

"Wow," said Fungus, "that was a narrow one. Thanks, Linda. I don't think I could have coped with that."

"Hell on wheels," agreed Haemar, who had followed Linda into the Chamber alongside Chris.

"Imagine. Playing in a band that uses a vibraphone. No wonder they call it hell."

"What did I do to him?" wondered Linda.

"Basically," Lakin told her, his eyes not moving from Ned, "that spell you cast bound the Demon Melgior to work on the tills at Habitat for a year."

Fungus and Haemar looked at each other.

"Bit strong, even for a vibraphone player," they agreed.

Ned reached out for the Amulet, but Lakin's sword slammed down on the Altar in front of him. Sparks flew when the sword met the Stone. Ned looked around wildly, but his hopes (like the FireTroll) had fled. Chris walked around to the back of the Altar to see the Amulet better.

"How did you find it?" Lakin asked Ned. "How did you know where to look, when we had searched the Helvyndelve for an age without success?"

"The Grey Mage was at the gig, that night when Lucan did a runner."

"He did not do a runner, as you put it. He vanished in mysterious circumstances."

"And so did a lot of other stuff, and a couple of very tasty looking witches according to the Grey Mage."

Lakin seethed. "He was Archlord of Helvyndelve. Why would he abandon all that?"

"Let's see," answered Ned. "On one hand, he has the control of a big, but underground mansion, with nothing to do but listen to Radio One or occasional gigs by this lot. An' lots of dwarfs all complaining. And every time he sticks his head outside he gets it wet in the rain. On the other hand, he has a couple of nice girls, a lot of cash, and he's somewhere warm and sunny, where the drinks are cheap. Hum. Which one might you choose?"

Even Lakin could see that the options were not as clear-cut as he had thought. "I would still chose my heritage," he said, but more thoughtfully than before. "Anyway, how did you know where the Amulet lay hid?"

"The Grey Mage got this Silver Compass."

"I've got a Silva compass," contributed Fungus.

"He hexed this one so that it would show me the way to any seriously magical source. And as the Amulet was the most magical thing in the Helvyndelve, the compass led me straight there."

Lakin sheathed his sword, and leaning across the Altar, reached out and grabbed the Amulet. He froze on the spot, as a golden glow began to surround him. All eyes turned to him except for Ned who grabbed Chris by an arm, and drew his knife.

"Stay still," he hissed into Chris' ear, "and you might live to see another MacDonalds." With one arm around Chris' neck, Ned started to back out of the Chamber, but headed for the left hand tunnel. Chris kept struggling, but the knife at his neck was a threat. Linda snarled in rage, causing Fungus to step smartly away from her, and moved forward.

"I know that you will be following me," Ned said, pausing only to lift the chain holding the Ward of Lingard over Chris' head, and dropping it awkwardly around his own neck. "I might not have the Amulet, but with this I can survive when I get back to our World. I know you will be following me. Do not get too close, or I might forget my promise to let this one live."

Ned thrust Chris out of the Chamber, and with the knife at Chris' back they left.

"What do we do now!" demanded Linda.

Lakin still seemed unable to move. Fungus looked around, emboldened slightly by his victory over the FireTroll. "You look after Lakin. I'm going after Chris."

"Fungus, that's very brave of you," exclaimed Linda.

"No, I'm still terrified. But I'm still more terrified of yer aunt than of him." Fungus slung his sax back onto his back, and crept out of the Chamber. The tunnel quickly twisted left, then to the right, and then changed into a long series of steps winding upwards. Fungus trudged upwards as fast as he could, trying to work out a conversion to sax for the great solo from 'Stairway to Heaven' as a means of keeping the existential dread from overwhelming him. Always the footsteps in the dust led on before him.

Back in the chamber, the glow surrounding Lakin faded out, leaving excess pleasing rainbow colours in the retina, very similar to the colours caused by the excess of alcohol in the retsina. Lakin slumped against the Altar, looking in need of the retsina. Linda looked nervous as the light faded, but then produced her ward and hoped for some light. Then she recalled the Word of Power. "Luthen," she said, firmly. At once the ward lit up, and light returned to the Chamber. Haemar looked around nervously, but in the absence of any other aid, he realised he would have to make an effort. He lifted Lakin's arm around his shoulders, and started to lift him. The Amulet still flared with a golden light, although all else around seemed dark. As Haemar lifted Lakin and the Amulet from the Altar, the Stone started to crumble and collapse. By the time they had reached the left hand tunnel, the Altar had gone. Behind them the tunnel by which they had entered the Mound had also fallen in, and dust and mortar drifted down upon their heads.

"I don't think we've got very long to get out!" panted Haemar. "Someone's used some dodgy mix in the mortar."

Linda agreed, and helped lift Lakin, who was slowly awakening. They staggered into the passage that they believed would take them out of the Dark Mound, and the roof of the Chamber fell behind them.

"Friday afternoon job," panted Haemar. "No quality control. Wouldn't last more than a couple of hundred years from the look of it."

"I think we'll be lucky if it lasts long enough for us to get out," answered Linda, and indeed the stairs ahead of them were beginning to look less stable.

Lakin was now starting to wake up properly, and clasping the Amulet, he looked around at the crumbling walls. "We need to get out!" he gasped.

Haemar and Linda exchanged a look.

"Talk about stating the obvious," panted Linda.

"Clearly leadership material," replied Haemar.

"Can the Power of the Amulet keep the stairway together?" Linda asked.

"I will try."

"There's nice."

Lakin frowned in concentration, and the stairs took on a more solid aspect. "Hurry." Lakin said curtly.

More stones fell behind them, and they all hurried. At last, they reached the arch at the top of the stairs, and staggered out of the Dark Mound, falling gladly onto the clean ground. As they did so, the Mound vanished leaving a puff of brick tinged smoke behind it.

"Cowboy builders," said Haemar, from the ground where he had fallen. "Here, what am I lying on?"

The sounds underneath the very solid dwarf turned out to be Ned.

"How did that happen?" Linda asked a rather smug looking Chris.

"Well, when we got to the top, he was so pleased he pushed passed me to get out. So I just hit him, and tripped him up. Then Fungus turned up and sat on him. After that, he didn't want to get up for a bit."

"An' then one of you threw a dwarf at me," complained Ned. He looked more closely at Haemar. "Here, these etchings on yer helmet... What's this one doing? Oh, I can see now. That's not possible. Or legal."

"Never mind," said Lakin, still shortly. (He had not grown in the last ten minutes).

He looked around in the dark. "Anyone here?"

"We're all here, Lord," called one of his guards from the wall. The stones around the circle were now the normal stone colour (dirty) and no longer shone with an inner light, so it was less easy to see the dwarfs surrounding the Circle. Hence an improvement, on more than one level.

"What's going on, do we have any idea?"

"No. A small force of Bodgandor went past about an hour ago, heading for the Doors, and we have been hearing a pretty good fight going on that way, but that's all."

"Then I think that we need to go and find out," said Lakin.

"Don't we get a rest?" asked Fungus.

"Not much longer now. We'll have a rest at the Doors, and get food there."

"Food!" said Linda eagerly.

"Don't get too excited," warned Haemar. "The best the Door Wardens can manage is a greasy fry up. No healthy options at all."

Surprisingly, the news that food might consist of fried sausages, eggs, bacon, tomatoes, mushrooms, and a fried slice (and possibly a serving of oven chips) did not receive the horrified reaction he expected. Of course, as the lead singer, he was more careful of his throat than the others. Felldyke in particular held the opinion that this was a perfectly normal diet, and Scar held no objections either.

"Couple of you, bring him." Lakin pointed at Ned, who was promptly tied up. He complained a lot, until a very grubby rag was pushed into his mouth, and tied in place. He shut up quickly, for fear of being poisoned as well as squashed and bound.

Lakin led his assorted party across the fell side.

"Why does he keep calling it a party, when there's no booze?" asked Fungus.

They walked for an hour, and halted to rest upon the top of High Seat. When they let the gag out of Ned's mouth, he began to complain, so the teenagers sat upon him instead of the cold ground* Looking down into the vale, they could see the Edern ride into the valley, and watched the ambush by the Bodgandor.

*[After all, sitting on cold ground gives you piles. Piles of what is not normally mentioned, but it is a fair bet that it isn't gold.]

Shortly afterwards, all the dwarfs cheered as Erald and the dwarf army in turn ambushed the Bodgandor.

"Just like at the movies, isn't it?" remarked Fungus cheerfully. Chris nodded, but Linda disagreed.

"No popcorn," she objected.

"Come on, let's join in!" shouted Lakin. His guards were enthusiastic, the Banned Underground less so. Lakin pulled Fungus on one side.

"Listen, Fungus. Now I have the Amulet, when..."

"If."

"When."

"If."

"WHEN we win, I'll pay for a full gig for you. I'll throw in the lot, security, backstage freebies and goodies, catering, the works. I'll even cover all the ticketing, in case you don't sell enough. And pay for filming. Just this last one favour."

"What?" Fungus had a sneaking suspicion.

"Drag that Ned down behind us, so that the boys are free to fight."

"OK, you're on." Fungus picked up the rope that held Ned and turned to Scar, Felldyke and Haemar. "This is it, boys! The big one once that fight is over. And no management fees, all to us!"

"Now that's motivational speaking," Scar commented.

"Certainly motivated me," agreed Haemar.

"What's he on about?" asked Felldyke the drummer.

"Just keep hitting the skins, man."

"We talking drumming or fighting?"

"I'm surprised he can tell the difference," Scar whispered.

Lakin waved his sword, and the small group ran down the hillside, passing the tarn and heading for the battle. As they got nearer, an awful noise rose to the heavens, as though some metal monster was being tortured, and without any Americans present to make the use of illegal force legitimate.

Fungus went grey, instead of green. "That's the Bonnie." He choked. "I'd know that sound anywhere. MY BIKE'S IN DANGER!"

Fungus accelerated fast down the hillside, to the cheers of his compatriots (and complaints from Ned who was being towed behind him at an alarming rate). Fungus let go of Ned, who continued to skid down the hillside, until he stopped by banging into the bodies of his two colleagues from the Watches. Who hadn't been looking out for that and so received a pleasant surprise, albeit one travelling at fifteen MPH.

Fungus passed them without a second glance, or indeed a first glance, focussing his attention on his stricken joy. Without pause, he stuck out an arm and beheaded two Bodgandor who were creeping up on some Edern whose attention had been taken by the Bonneville and its progress. Fungus fell on the bike, then turned to look at Lugh. "Were you driving?"

"Yeah!" enthused Lugh. "It's fantastic!"

"It's a wreck!" howled Fungus, and promptly smacked Lugh on the nose so hard that the Tuatha flew across the bike, landing next to Finn (who took the opportunity to kick him). Fungus looked round. "And the Harley," he wailed, as Laeg skidded to a halt beside them.

"We've looked after it Fungus. We were just desperately in a hurry to get here, Look, there's only a small dent on the front mudguard where we ran over a Bodgandor. Or three. And the blood on the scuttle there will wash off. Diarmid made some marks on the pillion in the fight, but we'll make him clean it up."

Laeg looked at the defeated Triumph. "Grizelda will hex it back to life for you."

"But it won't be concours any more if she does that."

"But it will save you having to source a back mudguard. You know how rare they are."

Grizelda, after an emotional reunion with her wards, and the children, (All right Kids? Yes Auntie. Then we'll say no more about yer running off like that then.) came down to Fungus. "Since yer brought them back alive, Fungus, I'll make sure that the bike gets fixed."

Fungus was grateful, but convinced that Lugh ought to be made to pay.

Grizelda laughed. "I've thought of a way to do that."

On the other side of the valley, the few remaining Bodgandor slunk away and vanished into the mist.

"That's the last we'll see of them," said Grizelda

"Where's the Grey Mage gone to?" asked Finn, looking round.

"I'll go see." Grizelda climbed, rather stiffly, onto her broomstick, and lifted cautiously over the trees (in case some squirrels infringed her modesty). Minutes later, she was back, laughing.

"What gives?" asked Lakin, now wearing the Amulet of Kings openly about his neck and in consequence resembling a short John Travolta suffering from a Saturday Night Fever, and in need of a strong dose from Doctor Feelgood to restore his sanity.

"He tried to get away in a taxi. But the driver had let his badge lapse, and the car had no MOT. And it turned out that he was the owner. So they're all off down the Police Station for a while, and probably a large fine. Been taken away in a Black Maria."

"Didn't she have a walk on part in West Side Story?" asked Ben.

*

Slowly the Edern were reassembling their host. Lord Blear, once again calm and composed, rode over to the group. His eyes widened in surprise to see Lakin bearing the Amulet of Kings.

"I say, Old Chap, isn't that that Amulet thingy that Whatshisname, Lucan used to wear?"

"Yes, Lord Blear. I have recovered the Amulet of Kings."

"Mmmmmmmmmmmm," put in Ned, behind them.

"Stout work!"

"No, I think I've lost a little weight, actually."

"MMMMMMMMMmmmmmmm."

"Well, if you could let us have some hay and oats for the horses, and some food for the chappies who've been fighting here today, we can head off home to Sinadon. I have quite a lot of amendments to our constitution to propose, and a lot of work to do to ensure that my proposed reforms make it through at Board Level."

"MMMMMMMMMMMMMMMMM," said Ned, intelligibly. Of course, as no one had removed his gag, clearer communication was problematical.

"I think that I'd like to make some proposals." came a soft voice behind them. They spun round: to their shock there stood the Grey Mage, complete with his staff (the wooden stick kind, as opposed to the wooden stiff kind. OK, he had a couple of those as well, but they were not as important. No serious Evil warlock travels without his staff. And a couple of staff too.). One hand held the staff, the other Linda.

Ben shouted, and raised his own staff: but the Grey Mage made a mystical sign with his left hand, and Ben fell backwards, fighting for breath.

"The point is to have power at the right point," said the Grey Mage, pointedly. He looked at Ned, and prodded him with the point of his boot.

"Mmmmm," said Ned.

"Strange. He makes more sense with the gag in. Of course, the Tuatha would like to make a fight of it." He glared at Laeg who was casually trying to sneak into a position to attack from behind.

"Who? Us?" asked Diarmid.

"We only wanted to know the way to the pub," said Finn.

"It's the Red Lion, and it will only serve you if you have taken your boots off at the door," The Grey Mage advised, and then had to concentrate on Linda, who was fighting hard to get out of his grip.

"Stay still! Or I'll turn you into a frog, and drop you where the grass snakes live."

Linda went still. "Not MacDonalds, then?"

"Give me the Amulet, and I will let her go."

"You will let her go shortly, anyway." Grizelda sounded very calm. "How did you get away from the Police?"

"Simples. I just turned them into frogs, and jumped out when they crashed the police van."

"That is a bit antisocial," commented Finn, now looking at the sky behind the Grey Mage.

"MMMMM. MMMM.MMMMMM!"

"What are you all lookin' at?"

The Grey Mage spun round, and looked at the evening sky. The conference had finished, and the senior witches and warlocks of both Caer Surdin and Caer Rigor were returning home, bearing silly souvenirs, some happy memories and enormous hangovers. Some of the broomsticks were so overloaded that the owners had had to pay extra on the ferries, with the brooms being treated as an extra vehicle instead of hand luggage.

"Oh Damn it! Just when I thought I had won, too." The Grey Mage quickly turned on his heel, and vanished into the night, taking all his staff with him, and the three Watches as well.

"Wonder how he'll explain all this to his boss?" chuckled Finn.

"I expect he'll find a way to blame some one else. Important leadership skill that," said Blear, who knew all about that sort of thing.

"Corporate politics, eh?"

"Glad we don't have them, Erald."

"Is it opening time yet?"

"No, Finn. But we've got a few bottles back at the cottage."

Laeg went white. "I'd be careful, if I was you, Finn."

Epilogue

And two days later, they held the gig in Grizelda's garden. As promised, Lakin paid for the catering, to avoid Grizelda's cooking. Even the fridge came out into the garden, and was seen dancing with the man from the electricity company, before both vanished into the bushes.

Opening, as they normally did, with *'Going Underground'* before the crowd pleasers of *'Jailhouse Rock'* and *'Johnny Be Good'*. Why those two? Well, it's hard to think of two better songs for a live act to play to a drunken but appreciative audience. Just ask the bands that play at weddings (and at funerals, although the latter audience gets a bit too boisterous sometimes). After that, the Banned Underground got properly stuck in.

Dwarfs, Edern and Tuatha all got down to the serious business of having fun with enthusiasm. They even applauded Felldyke's drum solo, which goes to show.

As you might expect, the plants were enjoying the action too. "That bramble bush is really going for it," commented the foxglove to the rambling rose.

"I know, just cos that's a Rocking Berries cover."

A group of the revellers, headed by Linda, were inspecting the catering.

"What do you call that?" asked one dwarf, gingerly prodding a burger on the grill.

"George. Why, what do you think it should be called?"

Others had found Ben's remaining stash of bottles.

"What's in this?"

"Let's drink it and see."

"I'd advise against it."

"Why?"

"I drank one, and now I can't see properly."

Security too had been provided, but since no one in his right mind would try and gatecrash a witch's garden party, the guards were relaxing too.

"He's gone and done it again."

"Who?"

"What?"

"That Fungus. I swear he plays *At The Hop* to annoy me."

"Shut up, Marvin."

"Ned, do you think that they'll let us in?"

"Probably not."

"We could bring a bottle."

"We can hear from here. Most of Keswick will be able to hear from here."

"We could get the Environmental Health from the Council?"

"Won't work. The one who answers the phone is an AC/DC fan who just keeps saying Rock n Roll aint noise pollution."

Filming too was running into some obstacles.

"OW!"

"Well, look where you are going, then."

"Sorry. I can't see properly through the camera."

"Then try taking the lens cap off."

And the next day, when other people were doing the cleaning up and the goat was so full of discarded burgers that it could hardly move, Fungus, with Chris and Linda strolled back down the lane towards the cottage. They had been for a short walk to overcome the effects of the barbeque.

"I suppose that that is the end of the adventure," said Chris. "Now we can go home, as Aunt Dot tells us that our mum is out of hospital."

"Yeah," said Fungus. "Nothing to do now but watch the cleaners, eat a few mushrooms, and thank the author."

"What do you want to thank him for?"

"Well, he did give me a good gig at the end."

"I need to thank him," said Linda.

"Are you sure? It only encourages them."

"The whole book. And not one blonde joke. How did he manage it?"

"Probably forgot. You know what authors are like. So, back to Manchester now," said Fungus.

"Come and visit us?"

"I might just do that."

"Is that a promise, or a threat?"

"Which you would you prefer?"

"I'd prefer a curry after those burgers."

A small explosion lit up the garden, as the goat flew past.

"So did the goat."

ABOUT THE AUTHOR

Will Macmillan Jones lives in Wales, a lovely green, verdant land with a rich cultural heritage. He does his best to support this heritage by drinking the local beer and shouting loud encouragement whenever International Rugby is on the TV. A fifty something lover of blues, rock and jazz he has just fulfilled a lifetime ambition by filling an entire wall of his home office with (full) bookcases. When not writing, he is usually lost with the help of a satnav on top of a large hill in the middle of nowhere.

His major comic fantasy series, released by Red Kite Publishing, can be found at:

www.thebannedunderground.com

and information on his other work: horror and children's books and poetry and stuff in general at :

www.willmacmillanjones.com

There's a blog. There's always a blog, isn't there?

www.willmacmillanjones.wordpress.com

And Facebook
https://www.facebook.com/william.macmillanjones

And Twitter @macmillanjones

Printed in Great Britain
by Amazon